Just Say
Yes

LOOK FOR ALL THE BOOKS IN THIS
INSPIRATIONAL SERIES FROM BANTAM BOOKS.

clearwater crossing

Just Say Yes

laura peyton roberts

BANTAM BOOKS
NEW YORK • TORONTO • LONDON • SYDNEY • AUCKLAND

RL 5.8, age 12 and up
JUST SAY YES
A Bantam Book/March 2001

All scripture quotations, unless otherwise indicated, are taken from
the HOLY BIBLE, NEW INTERNATIONAL VERSION®. NIV®.
Copyright © 1973, 1978, 1984 by International Bible Society. Used by
permission of Zondervan Publishing House. All rights reserved.

Copyright © 2001 by Laura Peyton Roberts
Cover photography by Michael Segal
Cover art copyright © 2001 by Random House Children's Books

ISBN: 0-553-49332-9

Visit us on the Web! www.randomhouse.com/teens
Educators and librarians, for a variety of teaching tools, visit us at
www.randomhouse.com/teachers

Published simultaneously in the United States and Canada

Bantam Books is an imprint of Random House Children's Books, a
division of Random House, Inc. BANTAM BOOKS and the rooster
colophon are registered trademarks of Random House, Inc.
Bantam Books, 1540 Broadway, New York, New York 10036.

PRINTED IN THE UNITED STATES OF AMERICA

OPM   10   9   8   7   6   5   4   3   2   1

Above all, love each other deeply,
because love covers over a multitude of sins.

1 Peter 4:8

One

"I can't believe it's really starting!" Peter Altmann said to himself, hauling the brand-new Camp Clearwater flag up the pole near the center of camp. The colorful rectangle his mother had sewn fluttered in the early-morning breeze, two interlocking gold C's against a background of brilliant green. "The kids will be here any second!"

He glanced anxiously toward the trailhead where everyone would emerge from the woods after the rolling quarter-mile hike from the parking lot. Jenna Conrad and Chris Hobart, Peter's Junior Explorers partner, would be with the campers, as would Peter's older brother, David, who was driving the bus. Peter had reluctantly decided it was better if he skipped the bus ride and went directly to the campground on this all-important first Monday; someone needed to check the last-minute details and make sure everything was ready for the thirty-nine rambunctious six- to eight-year-olds who'd be attending his free summer day camp.

"Which means I'd better get moving," he muttered,

glancing at his new sports watch. His seventeenth birthday was still almost three weeks away, but his parents had given him the watch as an early present the night before. Not only was it waterproof, but it also had a stopwatch, which would come in handy for timing games and races.

Peter walked across the packed-dirt clearing at the heart of camp toward the refurbished pine-green cabin. He had been working with the Junior Explorers, the group he and Chris had started for underprivileged children, for nearly three years now, and a few of the kids had been with him the whole time. Many of them were from single-parent families, several were in foster care, and although most of them behaved most of the time, there were a couple of boys in particular that Peter could see using the stopwatch on before the summer was over. If they gave him too much trouble, he'd simply time them at sprints until they dropped.

At the edge of the woods behind the cabin, Peter inspected the contents of the adjoining lean-to cupboard built during a community work party.

"Everything's looking good here," he said, nodding happily as his eyes ran over the sports equipment Eight Prime had bought through its fund-raising efforts. It seemed hard to believe now that he and his seven best high school friends—Jenna, Miguel del Rios, Melanie Andrews, Jesse Jones, Leah Rosenthal, Nicole Brewster, and Ben Pipkin—had only met in the fall, forming Eight Prime after the unexpected death of a classmate had left them shaken and sad. Wanting to honor their friend, they had banded together to buy the Junior Explorers a bus in his memory. Since then, however, Eight Prime had taken on a life of its own, going on to raise more money for the kids and, most recently, to plan and staff Camp Clearwater.

Peter double-checked the three new lifeguard rescue tubes hanging on nails inside the lean-to, then closed the door with a smile. "I think we have it covered."

Another anticipatory glance at the trailhead revealed only trees, so he walked restlessly into the cabin. Inside the small one-room building, folding tables were already set up with craft supplies for the first day. Extra paints, brushes, and an inexpensive weather radio shared space on a windowsill. A stack of empty plastic crates against the back wall would store the lunches the kids brought from home, while plastic pitchers, paper cups, and packets of cherry Kool-Aid stood ready on a shelf for twice-daily juice breaks, something Peter's mother's had suggested to keep them all from getting dehydrated in the heat of a southern Missouri summer.

"I don't know how everyone's going to change into their bathing suits with all this stuff in here," Peter muttered worriedly, eyeing the big chunk of floor space the tables took up. Even in two shifts, one for the boys and one for the girls, dressing was going to be tight. He imagined someone getting a shoe caught inside a pants leg, losing balance, crashing into a craft table, and taking the whole mess to the floor.

Maybe Jenna should teach crafts outside on the benches. Or we'll fold up the tables before swimming. Or go to three—

Before he could pursue the thought further, shouts rang out on the trailhead, calling him outside.

"Peter! Peter!"

"We're here!"

"Yaaaaaaaaaay!"

Kids streaked out of the woods, some running across the clearing toward the cabin, others veering in the other direction, toward the flagpole, drinking fountain, and split-log benches. Beyond the benches, the lake sparkled in the morning sunlight, the short wooden dock stretching out invitingly from the shore.

Too invitingly, Peter realized as towheaded Jason Fairchild and his favorite sidekick, Danny, took one look and began sprinting directly for it.

"Jason! Danny! Stay away from the water!" Jenna shouted, jogging out of the woods behind them. Her cheeks were pink from the pace the kids had set, and strands of her long brown ponytail clung damply to her throat. Planting her feet near the end of the trail,

Jenna mustered more volume. "I mean it, you two. No one goes on the dock without a lifeguard!"

Peter smiled at the sight of his harried girlfriend. To him she was always beautiful, even with the cords standing out in her neck. Still, it looked as if she could use some help. Lifting his shiny new head counselor's whistle to his lips, Peter gave it a blast that froze thirty-nine kids dead in their tracks.

"Assembly!" he announced. "Everyone find a seat on the benches."

The campers started to move again, and soon a tennis-shoe stampede was converging on the center of camp. Dust boiled up, filling the air.

"They're out of control!" Jenna panted, running over to meet him. "I've never seen them this wild before. Not to mention so many of them at once!"

"They're just excited." He added a wink. "So am I."

David and Chris emerged into the clearing, and Peter knew that the rest of Eight Prime would arrive any second, driving separate cars. He clapped his hands for attention as he walked up to greet the kids clambering over the benches.

"Hi! Listen up, you guys! We're going to have a great time today, but first you have to sit down so I can split you into—"

"Look at me!" Jason cried, doing a balancing act on a fallen tree branch. His arms jutted out on either side, his feet creeping toe to heel as if he were on a high wire. "I'm the Great Jasoni!"

"You're going to land flat on your great hiney if you don't knock that off," Chris said.

Peter choked back a laugh.

Camp Clearwater was officially in session!

"Peter's going to freak," Melanie said again, unable to stop repeating herself. "We're already ten minutes late."

"Relax," Jesse replied from the driver's seat of his red BMW. The smile on his lips was lazy as he winked across the air-conditioned interior. "What's he going to do? Fire us?"

"Just because he isn't paying us to be counselors doesn't mean we shouldn't be on time. How's he going to handle all those kids by himself?"

"He's not by himself. Jenna and Chris and David were all supposed to ride the bus today, weren't they? Besides, he deals with some of those kids every weekend at the park—it can't be all that different."

"You're right," Melanie admitted, trying to calm down. The truth was that she'd have liked to be at camp early, to see the kids arrive. Jesse had been a couple of minutes late picking her up, though, and the time they'd spent making out in her driveway hadn't done anything to catch them up.

"Of course I'm right," he said, the same satisfied

grin on his perfect lips. "In fact, there's a turnout up ahead if you want to park for a while."

"Jesse!" she squealed, slapping his right arm. She could feel her cheeks turning red, more so because part of her would have liked to take him up on his offer. "You're terrible!"

"That's not what you said last night."

She rolled her eyes away from him, watching the fields pass by outside her window. They had both said a lot of things the night before, and it was still all so new, so strange, that she barely knew what to think. The hours after she had told Jesse she liked him were still kind of a blur. Although technically she hadn't told him she *liked* him. Not exactly.

If she closed her eyes, she could still see that moment in the Joneses' garage, the one when she'd told him she'd dropped Steve Carson simply because he wasn't Jesse. Jesse had seemed stunned for a moment, and then he'd grabbed her by one arm.

"Are you saying you *like* me?" he'd demanded.

"I'm . . . I . . . I might," she'd answered at last, afraid to say the things that were truly in her heart. She and Jesse had already tried once before, failed once before. She wanted to be with him so badly, but she felt faint at the mere thought of failing twice. If she said she loved him and things didn't work out . . .

As it had happened, she hadn't had to make any declarations beyond that first, faltering admission.

Before she could say more, Jesse had folded her into his arms, kissing her so passionately that she'd nearly forgotten how to speak anyway. About the only thing they had stopped long enough to establish was that Mandi, the girl Melanie had seen him with at the grad night party, was nothing more than a first date.

"Mandi's nice," he'd said between kisses, "but there's nothing serious. I mean, if there's even a chance with you . . ."

By the time Melanie had ridden her dad's old bicycle home from the Joneses' that evening, her lips had been chapped and her head spinning.

Spinning in a good way, she thought now, sneaking a sideways glance at Jesse. She'd been so swept away by her sudden change of fortune that she'd barely slept all night, and when she had she'd dreamed of being in Jesse's arms again, the sensation so real that she'd awoken with the feel of his fingers still warm on her skin.

"So how are we going to play this?" he asked abruptly.

"Play what?" she replied, startled to realize that the BMW's tires were already crunching through the gravel of the lake parking lot.

"This. Us." Jesse cocked a straight brown brow. "There *is* an us now, right? What do you want to tell people?"

"Nothing! I mean, uh, not *yet*," she added at the

sight of his clouding expression. "It just seems a little fast. And besides, it's the first day of camp. . . ."

He looked at her sharply, fixing her with intense blue eyes. A moment later he shrugged. "I guess I've waited this long . . . ," he muttered, climbing out of the car.

On the path through the trees they held hands, stopping for one last kiss before emerging into the clearing.

"I wish we could work together today," Melanie murmured, her hands still resting against his chest.

"I know. I don't know why Altmann is so hung up on separating everyone into girl and guy groups. The kids all play together at the park."

Melanie raised one shoulder. "Maybe that's the point. He wants camp to be different."

"Whatever," Jesse said, the word one long exhalation. "But we're spending tonight together. Right?"

She took a surprised step backward. "I don't think I ever said—"

"I didn't mean we were spending the *night* together." A suggestive smile crept onto his lips. "Not that I wouldn't like to."

"Slow down, Jones," she said, starting to breathe again. "That ship is so far from sailing you're not even on the dock yet."

"Can I at least buy a ticket?" he asked, grabbing for her again.

She skipped out of his reach. "No. But if you're

9

very, very good, I might let you show me your money."

She started for the clearing before he could respond, leaving him wide-eyed as he tried to guess her meaning. Flirting was like that. A girl said something off the top of her head, and if she was good—and maybe a little lucky, too—there would be several ways to interpret it, including one perfectly innocent one, the one she would later insist she had meant.

Melanie was good.

"Are you just going to stand there or what?" she added over her shoulder.

Jesse groaned behind her. "Wait for tonight," he warned, picking up the pace.

Melanie grinned. Tonight was *exactly* what she was waiting for.

"Cheryl, put down the glue," Leah ordered, raising her voice to be heard over the other chattering girls in her group. "The next person who puts glue anywhere but on a Popsicle stick isn't going swimming this afternoon."

"It's not *my* fault," Cheryl retorted from her seat behind one of the craft tables. "I don't understand this stupid project."

Leah gave her a skeptical look. "I'll bet you understand that it doesn't involve squirting glue at Lisa."

Lisa was still wiping the mess off her arm and

glaring nastily at Cheryl. She tossed perfect blond ringlets at Leah's words, vindicated.

"It's my fault," Jenna said worriedly, sniffing hard against a head full of congestion. "I should have started with something easier than these model birdhouses. The kids have been having trouble all day."

"No bird could ever live in one of these dinky things anyway," said Monique. "They're too little."

"They're *decorative*," Jenna said, sniffling again. The exhaustion in her voice made it clear she'd already explained that many times. "When we get them done, we'll paint them and glue on dried flowers. Won't that be cute?"

"I want to paint mine now," Amy Robbins announced.

Jenna squeezed her eyes shut, but when she spoke her voice was reasonable. "You can't. It isn't done yet."

"Then I want to paint something else," the little girl insisted.

"I'll make you kids a deal," Leah said, trying to regain control of the situation. "Whoever finishes her birdhouse first—and does it *right*—can have that package of M&M's I didn't eat at lunchtime."

"You promise?" Cheryl asked.

"All right!" seven other voices yelled.

Eight pairs of hands settled down immediately, completely absorbed in the task of gluing flat wooden sticks into a cube with a pointy roof. Leah couldn't help noticing that suddenly they all seemed to know what they were doing, too. She breathed a sigh of relief to finally see them quiet. They were cute girls, and she wanted to enjoy them, but they hadn't stopped talking once since they'd been assigned to her that morning. She'd already answered a million questions, everything from "Why do squirrels eat acorns?" to "How come you don't you have a middle name?" to "Why do we have to swim with the boys?" Her brain was exhausted.

And all she really wanted to think about was Miguel. And how much she loved him. And how close she had come the day before to ruining both their lives.

You knew Shane Garrett was bad news, she told herself. *You never should have gone to his dorm in the first place*.

Even so, she hadn't expected him to make a grab and try to kiss her in a public hallway. And she really hadn't expected herself to nearly let him. Shane's lips had been mere millimeters from hers— and hers had been puckered and waiting—when she'd abruptly broken his embrace, wheeled around, and run out of the building like a total lunatic. The whole encounter was so embarrassing that she still couldn't even think about it without cringing.

I'll bet Shane doesn't think I'm so mature now.

She had spent all Sunday evening waiting for him to call and ask what had happened. She had pretended to watch TV with her parents, her muscles so poised to spring at the first ring of the phone that she had actually made herself stiff. The call had never come, though, and she could only hope it wouldn't come today, because now that summer vacation had started, her college-professor parents were going to be home pretty much full-time until fall. In past years, one or both of them had taught summer classes, but this summer, Leah's last before she went off to college, they had decided to take a vacation in order to spend more time together as a family. Leah appreciated their intentions, but the last thing she wanted was for them to get involved in this mess—especially since her father actually *liked* Shane.

He won't call. If he didn't call last night, he's not going to call today. In fact, I'll be surprised if he ever speaks to me again.

She sighed, wishing she could be sure of that. From what she knew of Shane, giving up wasn't his thing.

The worst part was that, under different circumstances, she could have liked him. She could have liked him a lot, in fact. Shane was smart, good-looking, articulate, and going to Stanford in the fall, same as she was. But she was in *love* with Miguel. How could she have thought, even for a second, that she wanted Shane to kiss her?

"Where's Miguel now?" Jenna asked, making Leah jump with guilt.

She blinked a couple of times, studying Jenna's

face, before deciding the question was a coincidence. "Peter put him and Jesse in charge of the same group today, because tomorrow Miguel won't be here. He's got a day shift at the hospital."

Jenna nodded, glanced around to make sure the kids were still busy, then leaned casually against a wall. "I saw him yesterday afternoon. I was just out driving. You know. Picking up last-minute things for camp. Miguel was ... um ... out on the sidewalk of a street I drove down."

"Uh-huh," Leah said tensely. She had no idea if Jenna's story had a point, but she didn't like where it was heading. What if Jenna asked her why she hadn't been with Miguel? No way did she care to explain where she had been instead.

"Monique!" Leah exclaimed, hurrying around to the other side of the table. "You look like you could use some help with your roof. Should I hold that stick for you?"

The little girl accepted gratefully, but not everyone was pleased.

"No helping!" Priscilla shouted. "You're just fixing it so she gets the candy!"

"I hope being nice is more important than candy," Leah said preachily. "You should all be helping each other. Besides, if you help the person who ends up winning, maybe she'll share her prize with you."

Leah could see the candy calculators behind eight pairs of eyes clacking away like crazy before all the girls suddenly began trying to glue something onto any birdhouse but their own.

"Anyway," said Jenna, sniffing again as she tried to resume their conversation, "I saw Miguel and—"

"Are you coming down with something?" Leah interrupted. "You sound terrible." For the first time she noticed that Jenna's eyes were rimmed with red. "I think you're getting a cold."

Jenna fished a tissue out of her shorts pocket and blew her nose. "I *know* I'm getting a cold, but I'm trying to ignore it," she said miserably. "What I *don't* know is how I got it. I felt fine yesterday."

"Summer colds are the worst. You ought to go home now and try to shake it before it gets bad."

"Peter needs me. And besides, I want to be here. We've been planning this camp for weeks."

"But if you're sick—" Leah began.

"Done!" Cheryl shouted gleefully. "I'm done! Give me the candy!"

"Let me see," Jenna said, walking over to check. "Ooh, Cheryl, that's good!"

"No! No, it's not. She forgot the doorstep!" Priscilla said, still desperately gluing on sticks.

"Birds don't need a doorstep," Cheryl returned scornfully. "They don't walk. They fly."

"It's *decorative*," said Priscilla.

All the other girls started yelling their opinions, and soon Jenna was refereeing a full-out battle.

Note to self, Leah thought, *bribing the campers with*

15

candy might not be the best idea. She'd try to remember that in the future. For now, she was glad of anything that would take Jenna's mind off Miguel—and why Leah hadn't been out on the street with him Sunday.

The main thing is, nothing happened, Leah reminded herself for the millionth time. *I mean, not really. Nothing irreversible.*

Still, she didn't think she could be more ashamed even if it had. Miguel trusted her. She loved him. She never, ever should have gone to meet Shane.

Especially not after the heartache I gave Miguel about Sabrina Ambrosi. When I thought she was after him, I didn't shut up about it until he quit his construction job with her father. Leah sighed again, overcome with remorse. *Now it looks like I'm the one I should have been watching.*

There was only one positive thing about the whole mess: Miguel didn't even know Shane existed.

And he never will, she vowed, fishing the M&M's from her backpack. *If I told Miguel about Shane now, I'd look like the biggest hypocrite in the world!*

Two

Brrrrreeeeee!

Ben's whistle shrilled inside the moving bus Tuesday morning, louder than he had anticipated. Campers clamped their hands to their ears as the echoes ricocheted around the vehicle's metal interior.

"All right, children," Ben said into the shocked lull that followed. Every mouth had closed, every wide-eyed face was turned his way, but he still had to shout to be heard above the bus's noisy engine. "I think you all know that the correct way to ride in the bus is to sit down and face forward."

His voice came out unintentionally priggish, and the kids let him know it, snorting and sniggering. Ben was standing in the aisle near the first row of seats, facing the back, so he had a clear view of his mockers. For a moment he considered sitting back down—after all, it was only the second day of camp, and he wanted the kids to like him—but instead he wiped his palms on his multipocketed shorts, determined to prove he could be tough when he needed to.

17

"We can't have all this roughhousing and people out of their seats. It's not safe," he insisted.

Just then David hit a bump that launched Ben off the bus floor and sent him stumbling down the aisle. Gales of delighted laughter rang out as Ben narrowly avoided a face-plant by grabbing two seat backs. One knee grazed the rubber-matted aisle and then he was up again, but in that brief disturbance he'd lost the kids' attention.

Joey and Jason popped up over their seat backs to shoot spit wads at each other. Joey's aim was off; his sodden wad of tissue winged Lisa's cheek instead of hitting Jason. She immediately started squealing, launching two or three of the boys into high-pitched imitations, which made her even madder.

"You shut up!" she screamed. "I hate all you boys."

"Boys stink! Boys stink!" Priscilla called out gleefully. By the third repetition, all the girls had joined in.

"Boys stink! Boys stink! Boys stink!"

Not to be outdone, Jason led the chant for the other side: *"Girls bark! Girls bark! Girls bark!"*

The boys took this up with a vengeance, complete with wolf howls and *bow-wow-wow*s. The girls tried to shout them down while holding their noses pinched shut, skinny elbows high in the air. The racket was incredible—far worse than before Ben had intervened. He reached for his whistle again, just as Peter rose from his seat.

"That's enough!" Peter's voice cut the din like a scalpel. "If you can't respect each other, you can just be quiet until we get to camp."

Mouths closed. Heads hung. The only sound in the bus was the roar of the engine. Peter nodded and sat back down.

Ben stared at him, impressed. Peter hadn't used his whistle. He hadn't even yelled. He'd just told the kids what to do and they'd done it.

"And stay in your seats!" Ben added, pretending not to see Jason's tongue waggling in his direction as he stumbled back to his row.

Elton Carter, Ben's favorite Junior Explorer, was still saving Ben's half of the bench, facing forward and minding his business like a model camper. *Why can't they all be Elton?* Ben wondered, sinking down beside the chubby little boy.

"You shoulda been on the bus yesterday morning," Elton offered. "They're acting better today because *you're* here."

Ben smiled, even though he wasn't deluded enough to believe that. Peter hadn't been on the bus Monday morning either, and all a thinking person had to do was compare the way the kids reacted to Peter to the way they treated Ben and the actual reason for their slightly better behavior that Tuesday became clear.

"I like your whistle," Elton added, reaching out to touch it. "You didn't have that yesterday."

"No. I, uh . . . forgot it," Ben said, deciding that explanation was close enough. Elton didn't need to know that he had gone straight to the sporting goods store to buy it the evening before, having envied Peter his all day. David had a whistle too, since he was head lifeguard in addition to the bus driver, but none of the other counselors did. A whistle of his own was just the thing to make Ben stand out.

"Jenna's sick," Elton said, changing the subject.

Ben glanced back a couple of rows to where Jenna sat with one of the girls. There were so many used tissues on her lap that they had started spilling onto the floor, and her nose was chafed cherry red.

"You're right." Ben had noticed that Jenna was congested the day before, but nothing like this. As if reading his mind, Peter chose that moment to get out of his seat and walk back to his girlfriend's.

"Are you okay?" Ben heard him ask. "No offense, but you look pretty bad."

"I'mb fine," Jenna croaked, sounding anything but.

"What if you're contagious? Maybe you should go home."

"Who'll run the craffs if I do?"

"We could ask Melanie . . . ," Peter began.

"I'mb fine," Jenna insisted, blowing into another tissue. "You're already short Miguel today. You neebe."

"Well, of course we *need* you, but—"

"I'mb fine!"

20

Peter nodded and walked back to his seat, clearly still not convinced.

Ben did some quick calculations. Chris Hobart had helped out the first day, but he wasn't planning to be around much and was gone for the rest of the week. Miguel was working at the hospital, and David couldn't take his own group because he and the cell phone were supposed to hang out at the center of camp, to handle any emergencies. If Jenna went home sick and Melanie took her place leading crafts, they'd be down to five counselors for five groups.

Completely doable, Ben thought, not sharing Peter's concern. *Better, even.*

They had doubled up the day before, which meant Ben had had to share a group with Peter. With fewer counselors, he could be in charge of a group of his own. Jumping out of his seat, Ben hurried over to Jenna's.

"If you don't feel good, you should go home," he told her in his most sympathetic voice. "Don't worry, we can handle this."

"Rilly?" She looked up hopefully, her eyes glassy and half-closed.

"Definitely! With Peter in charge and me as second-in-command, what could possibly go wrong?"

Jenna's eyes opened a little wider, probably with gratitude. "Thanks, Ben. I'll, uh . . . tink about it."

Ben walked back to his seat, confiscating Danny's

peashooter on the way with one quick swipe of his hand. He heard Danny gasp behind him; the kid never saw it coming.

I'm getting better at this counselor stuff by the minute, Ben thought with a satisfied smile. *Heck, I could probably run the place without Peter.*

"I need you in 213," Howard told Miguel, ducking into the nurses' lounge. "The patient in there is crying, and I don't have time to calm her down. She's perfectly fine, just scared. Read her a story or something." The nurse was gone as quickly as he had appeared, the business end of his stethoscope bobbing over his shoulder.

Miguel sighed and put the time sheet he'd been filling out back into the slot where he kept it. His shift was over and he'd been planning to leave. But if Howard needed him in 213 . . .

Pushing back from the table he used as a desk, Miguel grabbed an armload of books and started down the hall. Sure enough, he heard a little girl whimpering even before he reached her open door. Checking the clipboard on the wall outside, Miguel learned that his charge was Amber, age four.

"Hello, Amber," he said, walking in.

Amber backpedaled in her hospital bed, thrashing with her legs until she had propelled herself up against the wall at its head. Her eyes were perfectly round, and the combination of those with her short red curls reminded Miguel of Little Orphan Annie. She stared at him in terror, her tears temporarily choked off by fear.

"Don't be afraid," he said, assessing the fresh cast on her arm. Kids didn't usually stay on the ward with broken bones unless there was something else going on. "I'm not going to touch you," he added as her legs continued to scramble.

"Where's my mommy?" the girl asked shakily.

Miguel had no idea. Some parents stayed in sight every minute until their child was discharged, even sleeping upright in uncomfortable chairs. But sometimes they had to work, or had other children they needed to take care of, or their kid was just in the hospital so long . . .

"I'm sure your mom will be back soon," Miguel said soothingly. "Did she have to go to work, maybe?"

Amber gave him a suspicious look. "I want her."

"I know." He took a seat far enough from the bed to prevent another freakout. The little girl relaxed visibly when she realized he wasn't coming closer.

"While we're waiting for your mom to get back, do you want me to read you a story?" he asked. "My name's Miguel, and I read to all the kids here."

He held up the books he'd brought so Amber could look them over.

"The spider," she said, pointing.

"All right. You're going to like this one," he said, putting the others on the floor. The younger kids went for the picture book about the lady spider and her friends at least half the time, which was why it rarely left his stack. He opened to the first spread, turning the pages toward Amber and preparing to read upside down over the top, a skill he had mastered through much practice.

"I can't see," she said with a trace of her former petulance.

"You could try moving a little closer," he suggested, pulling his chair in as well. Soon Amber had crawled back to a normal position in bed and Miguel was reading a story he could nearly recite without looking.

It's not that bad staying late, he told himself, trying to inject more enthusiasm into his reading. He had definitely been ready to leave for the day, but it wasn't as if he'd had plans. He'd just wanted time to think.

Or maybe to stop thinking.

Ever since Sabrina had laid that unexpected lip-lock on him Sunday, his mind had been racing like a rat on a wheel—around and around and around without getting anywhere. He was exhausted, and it would have been nice to have some time to compose himself before Leah got home from camp. He needed to be sharp if he was going to keep acting as if nothing was wrong.

Oh, well. He turned a page and continued reading. At least being there for Amber made him feel like less of a rodent.

Not that I invited Sabrina to kiss me.

The only reason he had even asked her to meet him on Sunday was to take her past Charlie's house and get her opinion on whether he should buy it. From a construction standpoint. Strictly professional. Sabrina was the daughter of a contractor and well on her way to taking over the family business someday, so he trusted her opinion. If Leah had shown any interest in his dream of buying that house, maybe he'd have taken her instead. But she'd made it perfectly clear she thought the whole idea was stupid.

Not as stupid as me telephoning Sabrina, he thought now, flipping another page. He'd been eaten up with guilt ever since the moment her lips had touched his. He'd barely slept the past two nights, wondering how he was going to tell Leah. Until, at some point, he had started wondering *if* he was going to tell Leah.

That kiss didn't mean a thing, he thought, *and it definitely won't happen again. I set Sabrina straight on that score.*

Of course, he had set Sabrina straight before. Apparently it hadn't stuck.

Which is why I'm going to avoid her. I'll just stay far away and we'll put this behind us and . . . oh, man. Who am I fooling? Leah is going to be furious!

Which is why I shouldn't tell her. Sabrina's sure not going to tell her, and no one else was there. Why make Leah mad by telling the truth when all I have to do is keep quiet? It's not like I'm lying. And I'm certainly not cheating on her. There must be times when it's okay for a guy to just keep something to himself.

"That's not what it says," Amber protested, breaking into his thoughts. "I've heard this book before."

Miguel double-checked the page and realized he'd skipped two lines. "Sorry," he murmured, backing up to start from the top.

"I still can't see good," Amber said, stopping him again.

"Well . . . do you want to let me sit on the edge of your bed now?"

She scooted over, making room.

Miguel settled carefully onto the mattress, giving Amber a clear view of the book. "Okay now? All ready?"

She nodded and he started reading once more.

I'm just not going to tell her, he decided. *It'll only turn into a crisis. Besides, there's no way she can find out if I just keep my big mouth shut.*

"Stop that screeching and put on your bathing suits!" Nicole Brewster instructed irritably. "This is the last time I'm going to say it."

She already had a headache from herding her group around in the heat all day, and the eight high-pitched voices bouncing off the walls of the cabin felt like ice picks in her ears.

"I can't tie my top," Belinda wailed.

"That's because you're too fat," said Meri. "The strings aren't long enough."

"Be-luuuuuuu-ga," Jordan brayed, setting off a chorus of giggles.

Nicole was inclined to agree. No eight-year-old ought to have that type of blubber. And no one so fat should even *consider* wearing a two-piece. But now the unfortunately named Belinda was starting to cry, which didn't help get Nicole's group to the lake for afternoon swimming.

"I'll tie it for you," Nicole said impatiently, grabbing the strings. "You other girls shut up and get dressed."

She knew she could have been nicer, but after nearly two days of camp she didn't feel particularly nice. All she did was sweat, make Kool-Aid, and play sports she didn't even like, while the kids just whined, whined, whined. Maybe if she had gotten some of the cute girls in her group, like Lisa and Amy, things could have been more fun. But when Jenna had gone home sick, Peter had shuffled everyone around and stuck Nicole with all the rejects.

Nicole pulled the bikini ties tight across Belinda's fat back, watching them sink in like the strings on a Christmas ham. "How's that?"

"Good," Belinda whimpered.

Nicole tied a knot, just to be safe. "All right, everybody grab your towels and get out of here," she shouted. "I want you all at the lakeshore pronto!"

Things were better once the kids got into the water and Nicole had staked out a good place to lie on her towel in the shade. She was free to go swimming too—David, Peter, Jesse, Leah, and Melanie were serving as that day's lifeguards and Ben was in the water, splashing around like the undignified fool he was—but Nicole had had enough of the kids for one day. All she wanted was a break.

A long *break*, she amended, disgusted to note that her new pedicure was already chipping from contact with so much dirt. Cheerleading camp would take her away all next week, but meanwhile Peter was expecting her to work the rest of this one. Three more days of screaming kids and sunburns and dust in every crevice of her body. Three more days of chapped lips and mosquitoes and poison ivy.

I ought to look great by the time I get to cheer camp, she thought sarcastically, wishing she'd remembered to bring a hat. *Bug bites all over my body, a nose like Rudolph, and calamine lotion up to my neck.*

A whistle shrilled from the dock, momentarily diverting her attention from the fingernail she'd broken that morning. Peter's brother, David, was waving his arms and yelling something to a group of kids in the water.

28

They're probably out too far or something, she thought idly, focusing on David instead. He looked like Peter, only older, more muscular, more blond, more handsome . . .

Who'd have guessed Peter's brother would be so hot? If Peter turns out half that good, then Jenna's a genius to grab him now.

Not that Nicole was interested in trying to get something started with David. For one thing, Jenna had already made sure everyone knew he belonged to her older sister, Caitlin. For another, Nicole had just broken up her on-again, off-again relationship with Guy Vaughn on Sunday. The last thing she wanted was anything serious.

At least not until fall, she thought, smiling.

Now that she was a cheerleader, she would have her pick of guys. In fact, they were lining up already. Saturday night, at the last graduation party she and Courtney Bell had gone to, Noel Phillips had asked for her phone number. Noel Phillips! She barely knew him, but everyone said he was going to be senior class president next year. On top of that, he was great to look at: dark brown hair and chiseled brows, a squared-off jaw, and the most melting hazel eyes—half green, half brown. Nicole felt woozy just remembering the way they'd slow-danced.

I wonder if he'll call me. She would gladly make an exception to her nothing-serious rule for Noel.

Another whistle. Peter's. This time Ben was being

waved out of the water. Nicole hadn't seen his transgression, but he was almost certainly the biggest menace out there.

What a way to spend my vacation, she thought. It wasn't that she objected to helping out. She just had a million other things on her mind: cheer camp, and what to wear to cheer camp, and shopping for cheer camp, and packing for cheer camp . . .

I ought to be getting ready right now. I could be putting my outfits together, buying new makeup, letting the swelling go down on these bites. In fact, what am I even doing here? Peter can figure out how to run this place without me until I get back. Meanwhile, what kind of impression am I going to make if I show up looking like I've been on Survivor?

The last thought made up her mind. Getting the other cheerleaders to accept her had been one heck of a rocky road, and she had just started to make some progress. She couldn't afford to blow it now by looking awful at cheer camp. Not stopping to think another minute, she jumped off her towel and strode purposefully down the shore to Peter.

"You're going to have to take me off the schedule for the rest of the week," she blurted out. "It turns out I'm going to be busy."

"Are you kidding me?" Lifeguards were never supposed to take their eyes off the water, but Peter did anyway. "Busy with what?"

"I told you. I have cheerleading camp."

"You told me that's *next* week," he said, a bit of panic in his voice. "I've got you off the schedule all next week."

"Well, I just found out I'm going to need some extra days. You can cover things without me."

"How?" he asked, as if that were her problem.

"Get Miguel. Or Jenna will probably feel better tomorrow. Anyway, this is my last day."

Peter suddenly seemed to remember he was supposed to be watching the kids. "Fine. Have a good time," he said acidly, returning his eyes to the water.

I will, Nicole thought as she walked off. Although she had to admit that sarcasm was the last thing she'd expected from Peter. It was so uncharacteristic, in fact, that he almost made her feel guilty.

Still. It was her vacation. And she had better things to do.

Much better things, she reminded herself. *Anyway, who died and made Peter king? I said I'd help—not give up my whole summer*.

By the time the kids finally climbed onto the bus for the day, Nicole had managed to dispel any lingering feelings of guilt. Later, driving home in her mother's car, she started to feel positively excited.

I should have thought of this yesterday! she congratulated herself, imagining the fun she and her best friend, Courtney, would have in a nice air-conditioned mall.

Things only got better when she walked in her front door.

"Who's No-*el*?" Heather demanded, accosting her in the entryway.

Nicole felt her heart skip a beat, even though her ignorant younger sister had just slaughtered the poor guy's name. "Who wants to know?" she countered.

"Mom left a message on the chalkboard. It says No-*el* called and a phone number. I don't know a No-*el*. Do you?"

Nicole could barely keep from screaming with joy. Instead she put on the most superior look she could muster and stared down her nose at Heather.

"His name is pronounced Knoll," she said. "It's French."

"That's a *guy's* name?" Heather asked disbelievingly. "Are you sure?"

Nicole brushed past her sister to check the message in the kitchen herself. Sure enough, Noel had left his phone number!

"Does he want me to call him back?" she wondered.

Heather snorted behind her. "No. He wants you to do numerology with his phone number."

"Who asked you, Heathen?" Nicole retorted. "Where's Mom?"

"At the store. And I'm going to tell her you called me that when she gets back."

"Oh, grow up! Are you going into high school, or kindergarten? 'Ooh, Nicole called me a name,' "

Nicole mocked, pushing past her again en route to the stairs. "Get a life, why don't you?"

"I'm going to tell!" Heather shouted with more conviction.

By the time she was halfway to her room, Nicole had forgotten that Heather existed. Noel Phillips had called her. Her!

Should I call him back now, or wait and pump Mom for details? I don't want to look too eager.

But she was. Way eager. Nicole's imagination was practically shorting itself out producing visions of herself in her cheerleading uniform, walking into the CCHS cafeteria on the arm of the senior class president. Talk about coming up in the world!

I hope he's going to ask me out!

The mere possibility made her fall backward onto her unmade bed, completely oblivious to her skin's sticky coating of insect repellent and dust.

Wouldn't that be something? Nicole and Noel. It even sounds good!

Three

"Is that nose of yours running for President?" Mary Beth quipped, laughing at her own joke.

Jenna shot her oldest sister an unappreciative look and saturated yet another tissue. Mary Beth had only arrived home from college the day before, and already her humor was wearing thin.

"Oooh, way to honk! Sorry, but the geese have already flown north for the summer."

"Very fuddy," Jenna said miserably. "I have a cold."

"No kidding." Mary Beth peered into the fruit bowl on the kitchen counter and selected a nectarine. "Why don't you go incubate those germs somewhere else?" she asked, washing the fruit under the faucet. "We have to eat in here."

Jenna glared at her sister a moment, trying to think of something clever to say, then reluctantly heaved herself off the barstool and put her tea mug in the dishwasher. She felt better in bed anyway, and since she'd been too sick to help out at camp that Wednesday she knew she should try to get well fast.

I hope Peter is doing all right without me, she

thought, shuffling in her slippers up the two flights of stairs to her bedroom. He had called the night before, in a total sweat about Nicole's bailing out on him. Having to tell him she wouldn't be back for a day or two either hadn't been the easiest thing Jenna had ever done.

"I'mb rilly sorry," she'd forced past the congestion in her head. "I wish I could comeb, but—"

"No. That's okay," he'd said. "Just stay home and get better. Get better *fast*, all right?"

"I'll do by best," she'd promised.

Now, halfway up the stairs, she wished she'd thought to bring a pitcher of orange juice with her. Vitamin C was supposed to be good for fighting a cold. But she was nearly to the third floor, and the juice was way down on the first. . . .

I'll drink some at lunch, she compromised, too dizzy to make the trip.

Back in her bedroom, she crawled under the covers despite the continuing heat wave outside. She'd been freezing all morning, which probably wasn't a good sign.

"I can't believe I had to get sick *dow*," she groaned to no one. Caitlin had long since left for her job at the vet's office, taking her skinny dog, Abby, with her. "Dis is da pits."

The only good thing about it was that she wouldn't have to face Miguel again. She had barely been able to look at him Monday, knowing what she did about him and Sabrina Ambrosi. It made her sick to think he was such a snake—and that she had so totally misjudged him. If she hadn't seen with her own eyes Miguel kissing Sabrina, she never would have believed he could cheat on Leah.

I wish I'd never taken that wrong turn, she thought for the millionth time. Flopping onto her side, she punched at her pillow in an attempt to get comfortable. *If I hadn't been driving in the wrong part of town, I still wouldn't know a thing.*

It killed her to have a secret so big and not be able to tell anyone. She wanted to tell, she was *dying* to tell—but who?

Leah, that's who, she thought, groaning again. Jenna had tried to clue her in on Monday, but for an intelligent girl, Leah had been surprisingly dense. All Jenna's hints had gone nowhere, and the thought of actually coming out and *saying* Miguel was cheating was too horrible to consider. On the other hand, didn't her friend deserve the truth?

I wish I knew what to do. Dear God, if you could please help me out with this, or at least steer me in the right direction . . . I want to do what's right, I just don't know what it is!

A sudden burst of "Chopsticks" from downstairs told Jenna that Sarah was back on the piano. The youngest Conrad had taken a sudden interest in learning to play over the summer, but so far all her practicing had only increased her volume. Jenna pulled a pillow over her head as the tortured chords pounded at her eardrums.

As if to add insult to injury, Maggie chose that moment to laugh raucously in her second-floor bedroom. The sound was enthusiastically echoed by her newfound trio of best girlfriends, their laughter eerily similar to hers. Jenna wondered what her other younger sister, Allison, was doing, since Maggie had no doubt banished her from their room again. Ever since Maggie had formed her exclusive new clique, she didn't have the time of day for anyone else. With her freshman year of high school looming on the horizon, suddenly all she cared about was being popular.

Maybe I should tell Peter about Miguel, Jenna thought, shutting her ears against the noise.

Immediately she remembered the time she had told Peter about Caitlin's crush on David—and what a mess that had turned into.

This is between Leah and Miguel, a little voice said.

Then why do I have to be in the middle of it? she retorted.

The stress was killing her. In fact, it was probably the reason she'd caught a stupid cold in the first place. Leah was sure to break up with Miguel the instant she found out; she was far too proud to take something like that lying down.

The phone on the bedside table rang. Jenna dove for it, eager for the distraction.

"Hi, Jenna," Caitlin said. "Are you feeling any better?"

"Not rilly," Jenna told her forlornly. "By head's full of snot, Baggie's little friends are driving be crazy, and Sarah's on da piano again."

Caitlin's chuckle was full of sympathy. "Well, I can help you out with the last thing, at least. We're slow here and Dr. Campbell is giving me the afternoon off. I thought I'd take Sarah swimming up at the lake."

"Take Baggie too," Jenna begged.

"I don't think that's a good idea. Sarah's supposed to swim, but we don't want to disrupt camp with our whole family. Besides, I have to keep an eye on Sarah."

And David, Jenna added silently, smiling to herself. Sarah was just starting to walk short distances without a cane after the car accident that had almost killed her. Her physical therapist had upped all her exercises for the duration of summer vacation and had added swimming to the list. The idea was to build Sarah up to the point where she'd be able to return to school in the fall with only a limp.

"Just get here soon, den," Jenna begged.

"I'll try. Is Mom back from work yet?" Mrs. Conrad had gone to church that morning to try out some new arrangements for the choir.

"Un-uh," Jenna croaked.

"Then tell her when she gets back, okay? I've got to go, but I'll see you soon."

The phone went dead. Jenna flopped back into her pillows and drifted off to sleep.

"Jason, stop flicking pudding right now," Peter ordered sharply. "Louis, stop squirting juice or you'll both sit out during swimming."

"We're just trying to have some *fun*," Jason complained. "All day long around here it's 'do this' and 'do that.' When can we do what *we* want to do?"

"Never, if it's starting food fights." Before Peter could say more, a long, shrill whistle diverted the kids' attention.

"Everyone, listen to Counselor Ben!" Ben shouted from the bench he was standing on. Peter closed his eyes and stifled a groan.

The whole camp was eating lunch together that day, sitting on the split-log benches beneath the flagpole. With Jenna and Nicole both out and Melanie directing crafts, they had just enough counselors left to cover the five groups—which meant Peter had had to give Ben a group of his own. He had rearranged everyone to pick out the most docile boys for Ben—Elton, Jamal, Brendan, and the like—and he'd had to give Miguel a group of girls. Since Miguel couldn't help a bunch of little girls into their bathing suits, though, Melanie would have to take them over during swimming, when there were no crafts anyway. Miguel could lifeguard then, and Peter was hoping it would all work out. The entire morning had been one big stress fest, and now, just when things were finally settling down, Ben wanted to make a speech.

This can't be good, Peter thought.

Ben's whistle shrilled again. "Pay attention! Counselor Ben is speaking!"

Making all the kids call him Counselor Ben had been Ben's brainstorm of that morning. He thought the title would inspire the respect he hadn't been getting so far. Mostly it was inspiring snickers, especially when he used it to refer to himself in the third-person.

"Okay, here's what Counselor Ben is thinking," Ben announced. "Since we're all together now, we ought to sing some camp songs. It can be like a new tradition for us."

The kids greeted this idea with groans and shouts of "No!" while Peter massaged the new wrinkles forming in his forehead. He kept telling Ben that traditions had to develop on their own, but the guy was determined to make one happen through sheer willpower.

"That's what we're lacking. Tradition," he had lectured Peter at the morning assembly. "*Traditions* are the glue that holds the camp fabric together. If we had a few good *traditions*, the kids would get with the program."

Now Ben blew his whistle again to cut through the continuing chorus of disapproval. Kids clapped hands over their ears and kept yelling.

He's about two more blasts from getting that thing wrapped around his neck, Peter thought darkly.

None of the other counselors had a whistle—and they weren't supposed to, either. Peter had one as head counselor and David had one as head lifeguard, and those two would have been plenty. An overused whistle lost all effect. The way Ben overused it, someone was likely to lose an eardrum as well.

"Okay, here's the song we're singing," Ben announced. " 'Row, Row, Row Your Boat.' "

"That's a baby song!" Blane protested.

"Right, okay," Ben said, obviously scrambling. "But we're going to sing it in rounds. *Ha!* I'll bet you never sang it in rounds."

The kids who had finished their lunches gave Ben a little more attention. The others continued eating, completely ignoring him.

"First we'll sing it regular, just for practice," Ben told them. "*Row, row, row your boat* . . . Come on, everyone! *Row, row, row your boat* . . . Peter! Sing with us!"

"I can't carry a tune to save my life, Ben. I told you that this morning, when you wanted to sing at assembly."

"Oh, yeah. Right. Jesse, then. And Melanie! *Row, row, row your boat* . . ."

Through sheer persistence, Ben eventually managed to lead most of the campers through the song. Encouraged, he divided them into groups to sing in rounds. He had just cued the first group when Elton Carter put down his sandwich, looked directly at Peter, and threw up all over his own boots.

"Way to go, Elton. My thoughts exactly," Jesse joked as Peter rushed over to take care of the boy.

All the campers stopped singing and started screaming instead, most of them scrambling to get as far from Elton as possible.

"Ooooh!"

"Gross!"

"That *stinks!*"

Kids held their noses while they hollered, even the ones who were too far away to smell anything.

"Are you all right, Elton?" Peter asked, squatting down beside him. "Do you feel like you're going to throw up again?"

Elton looked from the vomit to Peter with tears pooling in his eyes. "I want to go home."

"Are you sick? Or was it something you ate? What's the matter, Elton? Tell me."

"I want to go home," the boy repeated, beginning to cry. "I want to go home right now."

"I'm sorry, but you can't. We don't have anyone to drive you. Maybe if you just lie down for a while . . ."

Elton cried more loudly.

Leah walked over, looked at the ground, and

shook her head. "You'd better send him home right now."

Peter could feel the panic starting again. If he had to send someone home with Elton, he'd be even shorter on staff. "He probably just swallowed wrong or something," he said desperately.

"Yeah. But what if he's really sick and we keep him here and he gets worse? We could all end up in a lot of trouble."

She was right.

"Is anyone even at your house?" Peter asked Elton. "I thought your mother was working."

"My sister," he snuffled. "She can watch me till Mom comes home."

"How old is she?" Leah asked.

Elton wiped his wet eyes. "Fourteen. I want to go home."

Peter nodded. "Ben!" he called, not realizing that Ben had already walked up behind him.

"What?" Ben shouted back, nearly giving Peter a heart attack.

Like my nerves aren't stretched thin enough . . .

Still, there was one way to turn this lemon into lemonade.

"Counselor Ben, I need you to drive Elton home. You've got a car today, right? Make sure his sister is there, and don't leave unless she is. Got it?"

"Got it!" Ben said, snapping off a salute. "Except who's going to take my group?"

"I will. We'll switch Melanie to Miguel's girls, then pool all the boys together for a game of baseball or something. We'll make it work somehow."

"I can come back after I take Elton home," Ben offered.

"Thanks, but don't bother. It'll be late by then, and we have David to help us with swimming."

"Well," Ben said slowly. "If you're sure you can manage without me . . ."

Peter helped Elton to his feet and gently pushed him in Ben's direction. It took every ounce of self-control he had to find a nonsarcastic smile. "Thanks. Like I said, we'll figure it out."

"How are you feeling now?" Ben asked nervously, cruising down the last main street before Elton's house. It was a lucky thing Ben had driven to camp that day instead of riding the bus, but his luck was sure to change if anything happened to his mother's car. "You're not going to barf again, are you?"

Elton shook his head. "Why do you keep asking me that?"

"The truth? Because my mom'll kill me if you get sick in here. If you think you're going to puke, at least stick your head out the window, all right?"

"I already said I would," Elton muttered. He didn't sound too cheerful, but a fairly normal color had returned to his cheeks.

I'll bet it was too much running around in the sun, and

maybe some bad mayonnaise. He'll be fine, Ben decided, preparing his explanation for Elton's mother. Elton's parents were divorced, and Peter had said the main reason Elton was in the Junior Explorers was to interact with other guys. Apparently his father didn't come around anymore.

"Hey, Elton? Bud?" Ben said, noticing two small boots heading for the dashboard. "Let's keep our feet on the floor mats, all right? I'll appreciate that."

They had hosed Elton's shoes down before they'd left camp, but the sour smell filling the car told Ben the boots hadn't come completely clean—definitely not clean enough to be up on Mrs. Pipkin's pristine dashboard. Ben was happy to drive his favorite camper home, but he'd be a lot happier if paying for professional auto detailing didn't turn into part of the deal.

Elton gave Ben an exasperated look and put his feet back down. "Turn here," he said, pointing. "That's my house."

Ben parked at the curb in front of a modest one-story with a white picket fence and flower beds full of color. He handed Elton and his backpack out onto the sidewalk, then trailed the boy up to his blue front door.

"You don't have to walk me," Elton said.

"I'll just make sure your sister's home. You don't want to end up alone all afternoon."

Elton shivered as if the idea hadn't occurred to

him and slipped his hand into Ben's. They stayed that way until Elton let go to put his key into the lock.

"Sis! I'm home," he shouted, pushing the door open.

"Elton? What are you doing here?" a girl's voice called back from deep in the house.

Elton walked into the living room, leaving the front door open behind him. Ben hesitated on the doorstep, not sure if he should follow the boy inside or wait to be invited. He was still standing there, deliberating, when a tall, skinny girl dashed around the corner, wearing shorts and a flowered tank top. The combination of her lanky body with her light brown hair and eyes made her the physical opposite of Elton in every obvious way.

"Oh," she said, catching sight of Ben and stopping short. "I, uh, I didn't . . ." She tucked her short hair nervously behind her ears, waiting for some sort of explanation.

"Elton got a little sick at camp today," Ben said, instinctively deepening his voice in an effort to sound more mature and responsible. "He threw up, so we thought we'd better bring him home. I think it was just the heat, or maybe his sandwich didn't agree with him."

"I made that sandwich!" she cried, stricken. Her eyes were wide and, Ben couldn't help noticing, pretty. "Elton?" She turned to question her brother, but he had disappeared into the house.

46

"It probably wasn't the sandwich," Ben said quickly, hating to see her upset. "He's fine now. Really. I don't think there's anything wrong with him at all. In fact, if you hadn't been here, I'd have taken him back to camp."

He realized he was running off at the mouth a bit but found himself unable to stop. Elton's sister was cute. Really cute. Ben couldn't have said whether it was her pink toenail polish, the cuff of beaded bracelets she wore, or the glittery bobby pins in her short hair, but there was something about her that was just so sweet, and innocent, and . . . *girly*.

"Okay! So I'll be going now," he said, abruptly self-conscious. "Tell your mom to give Peter a call if she wants to keep Elton home tomorrow. Otherwise, we'll expect him on the bus."

He started to walk away, but she called out after him.

"Wait! You didn't tell me who you are."

He faced her again, feeling rather foolish. Somehow, though, he managed not to show it.

"I'm Ben," he said coolly. "Ben Pipkin. The kids call me Counselor Ben, but that's because . . . well, you know. They see me as an authority figure."

She nodded. "Oh, sure. Elton talks about you all the time. You go to CCHS, right?"

"Right," he said, surprised. "I'm, uh . . . I'm a junior, actually."

"I'm going to be a freshman this fall. My name's

Bernie, but I guess you already know that. From talking to Elton, I mean."

Ben did some quick thinking and decided against revealing the fact that Elton had never mentioned her, maybe because she just looked so darn cute standing there. Even her *knees* were cute. . . .

"Bernie," he repeated, knowing it would be a long time before he got her name out of his head. "Well, I guess I'll probably see you at school, then."

"Yeah. If we don't run into each other again before that."

Was there something hopeful about the way she said it? Or was that wishful thinking on his part?

"Yeah." He tore his eyes from her all at once, hurrying for his mom's car before he could mess things up.

On the drive home he had to admit it, though. Bernie Carter was way too cute for him. Once she started high school, all the other guys would find out about her and she wouldn't give him the time of day. Right now she probably thought he was some sort of cool older guy, but when she got to CCHS and found out what a rep as a geek he had she'd—

"Wait a minute," he said slowly, the beginning of a plan forming in his mind. "What if she *didn't* find out? At least, not right away?"

After all, fall was a long way off. If he could make a good impression on Bernie *now*, before she found out what he was really like, then maybe—just maybe—he could actually get something started.

Wouldn't that be great? he mused. *Starting my junior year with a girlfriend?*

Part of him, the sane part, knew the entire idea was crazy. He and Bernie didn't even know each other. Maybe they wouldn't even *like* each other. It was way too soon to be thinking of her as a girlfriend. It was probably too soon to be thinking of her as a date.

But the other part, the love-at-first-sight part, just kept on smiling.

You never know unless you try.

Four

"Here. I made you some of that powdered lemon-ade from the cabin," Miguel said, handing Leah a paper cup. "It's not that great, but you might as well drink it, as hot as it is today."

"Hey!" Mickey protested. "Where's ours?"

"You know where the drinking fountain is," Miguel told him, pointing to a spot under the nearby oak. With Nicole and Jenna still missing from action, the kids were all eating together on the benches again that Thursday, a system they seemed to enjoy more than staying in separate groups anyway.

"I want lemonade too," Joy said.

Leah smiled guiltily as more girls clustered around her. "I'll make you all some at juice break this afternoon."

They seemed content with the promise, especially since they already had drinks in the lunches they'd brought from home. Suki even scooted over on the bench so that Miguel could have the seat next to Leah.

"Don't you have to sit with your boys?" Leah asked, surprised.

Miguel shrugged and glanced back over his shoulder. "Peter and Jesse have things under control."

Leah looked as well, and saw most of the boys playing a game that seemed to involve pushing each other off the benches into the dirt—last one standing won. Some of the more adventurous girls had joined in too, with plenty of squealing and shouting.

"I guess control is relative," she said dryly.

"It is around here. So what do you want to do this weekend? Should we go out Friday night?"

"You don't have to work?"

He shrugged again. "I got off. I know you've been wishing we could spend more time together, and that's what I want too. Hey, why don't we go to the Mapleton drive-in? That would be cool in your new convertible."

"Um, sure. That sounds fun." Leah took a big bite of her peanut butter sandwich, mostly to give herself the excuse of chewing while she tried to compose her thoughts.

She couldn't get over the change in Miguel. The week before, when they'd been graduating from high school and she'd been dying for his attention, he'd made her feel as if she had to beg for five minutes of his time. This week, when the Shane incident had left her too ashamed to look him in the eye, he was sticking to her like glue. Was it possible he'd guessed something was up? Or was it only her own guilt making her feel like she was under a microscope?

"How's that lemonade?" he asked. "You haven't even tried it yet."

She took a big gulp, washing down a lump in her throat that was only half peanut butter. The drink was lukewarm, with a bitter aftertaste. "Good," she lied.

Miguel leaned closer and smiled. Even with campers all around them she was right on the verge of confessing everything when an especially ear-splitting scream spun them both around.

Lisa Atwater was screeching, both hands clamped to ringlets dripping what looked like chocolate milk. The liquid rapidly stained her white T-shirt, seeping down to her yellow shorts.

"Jason!" Melanie scolded angrily. "Did you do this? Why do you always have to be so nasty?"

Jason ran around whooping it up, making all the other boys laugh too as Melanie put her arm around Lisa.

"You are in a lot of trouble," Melanie told Jason. "Whose group are you in today?"

"Oops," said Miguel. "I'd better get over there."

He left in a hurry, but not fast enough to avoid receiving a put-out look from Melanie. "I think you need to pay more attention," Leah heard her say before walking Lisa over to the hose for a makeshift shower.

Miguel cornered Jason for a little heart-to-heart that almost certainly included the loss of that day's swimming privileges, and Leah breathed a sigh of relief. She had been so close to telling him about Shane. . . .

And that would have been a big mistake.

How can I ever tell him? Not after the fits I threw about him hanging out with Sabrina! The only reason I even want to is to ease my own guilty conscience.

Certainly no good could come of it from Miguel's point of view. His feelings would just be hurt for no reason.

So it would actually be selfish not to keep it to myself, she thought, nodding. *Looking at it that way, I definitely shouldn't tell him.*

"Leeee-aaaah," Chelsea whined, crawling into her lap. "I'm bored."

Startled back to the present, Leah pulled the squashed remnants of her PB and J out from in between them. "Did you eat all your lunch?"

"We all did," said Joy. "We want to go swimming."

"Except that you know swimming doesn't start for a couple of hours," Leah countered, before the whole group could chime in. "How about a nice nature hike?"

"Noooooooo," they groaned in unison.

"It's too hot," Chelsea said, twining her arms around Leah's neck and pulling down with her whole weight.

"It's nice and shady under the trees," Leah said, untangling herself.

"Crafts!" Kelly bargained. "We could do crafts."

"Except that it's not our turn." Leah stood up and used a paper napkin to wipe most of the squashed sandwich off her shorts. "Come on. Maybe we'll find a bird's nest or something."

The girls picked up their trash and fell in behind her, but not without a lot more grumbling. Leah herself didn't feel much like hiking, but that was what Peter had written on her schedule, and as chaotic as things had been so far that week, she didn't want to knock him for any more loops. Leading her campers off across the clearing, she snuck one last look back at Miguel, who was just finishing his discussion with Jason. He seemed to feel her eyes on him, instantly turning her way.

"Bye!" he mouthed, waving.

Leah waved back, managing a weak smile before dropping her gaze to the dirt. Why did he have to be so nice *now*, she wondered, when she deserved it least? If he'd been this attentive the week before, she would never have gone to see Shane in the first place.

Life's not fair, she decided, heading for the trail. *And sometimes I think it messes us up just for the heck of it.*

"The best part of camp is after everyone else goes home," Jesse said, wrapping his arms around Melanie from behind.

"Mmm," she agreed, leaning back into his embrace. They were standing out on the end of the dock, watching the shadows lengthen across the lake. The day had been hot and hectic; now the evening stretched before them, calm and cool. "It's pretty out here, isn't it?"

Not that scenic beauty was the uppermost thing on Melanie's mind. Over the past four days, she had come to look forward to these first few moments alone with Jesse so much that they tantalized her all day, like the promise of an oasis on a long trek through the desert. Being a counselor was fun, although a lot more work than she'd expected, but it was torture being separated from Jesse all day— seeing him only from a distance, pretending he didn't matter to her one way or the other . . .

That was how they still played it. Except that sometimes their gazes would intersect and lock, and she couldn't believe the entire camp didn't know what a phony she was.

"What should we do tonight?" he asked.

Melanie wriggled around to face him. "What do *you* want to do?"

"Well, we can start like this."

He kissed her long and softly, his mouth melting into hers. She clung to him, so happy and relieved to finally be together that tears burned behind her lashes, and when at last his lips left hers she felt like she was falling.

"We can end like that too, if you want my opinion," she said, snuggling deeper into his arms. "Why don't we stay right here?"

"We might get pretty hungry." Dropping his hands to her waist, he set her back at arm's length. "Let's go to Slice of Rome. I'm dying for a pizza."

Melanie made a face.

"What?" he said. "You don't like that place?"

"It's okay."

"Then what?"

"I just . . . why don't we drive through somewhere again? It'll be a lot faster."

He gave her a quizzical look. "I didn't know we were in a hurry. Besides, I'm sick of eating in the car. Come on, let's have a pizza. It'll be fun."

Melanie shook her head. The reason they couldn't go to Slice of Rome was so obvious; did she really have to say it? She gave him a meaningful look. He stared back blankly. Apparently she did.

"That place is such a hangout. Someone is sure to see us," she said at last.

"So what if they do?"

"Jesse! The rumors will be all over town within twenty-four hours."

He let go of her. "And that bothers you."

Yeah, it bothered her. Big-time. It would be painful enough if things didn't work out between them—having the whole world in on the breakup could only make it hurt worse.

56

"It's not that it *bothers* me so much as—"

"What are we doing here?" he interrupted.

"What do you mean?"

"You and I. What are we doing?"

She tried to put her arms back around him. "If you don't know, you sure fooled me," she said huskily.

His body stayed stiff against hers; his arms didn't complete her embrace.

"No, I'm serious," he insisted. "If we're together, then let's tell people. Why are we sneaking around?"

"We're not sneaking around," she said, not understanding his hurry. Jesse had as much to lose as she did. There was no doubt he had as much pride. But for some reason he was in a huge rush to announce their relationship—and he had been ever since Sunday. Maybe he thought making things public would make them more real. It definitely raised the stakes.

Which was exactly what she was afraid of.

"Just a little longer," she begged, tilting her face up toward his. "Can't we let things happen on their own?"

His arms closed around her at last. "What do you want to do now, then?"

"Well," she said slowly, relieved, "I know a vacant poolhouse with a wide-screen TV. And I know a pizza place that delivers. We could rent some movies and hang out. Just you and me, all alone on that big, soft sofa . . ."

"All right, all right, you convinced me," he said,

smiling again. "You *more* than convinced me, in fact. Are you sure it's cool with your dad?"

"Pretty sure." The only reason it wouldn't be was if he was already in there, drinking. "If, uh . . . if my dad needs the poolhouse for some reason, we can always use the den," she added. Just because she and Jesse were together now didn't mean she intended to tell him *everything*. Her father's alcoholism, for instance, was one little secret she'd take to her grave.

"Sounds good to me." Jesse's arms tightened until he could swing her around him like a child, her feet barely skimming the boards as the lakeshore made a dizzy circle on her horizon.

And then he kissed her again, making her dizzier still.

"I'm really glad you called me when you did," said Nicole, "because I'll be at cheerleading camp all next week. Camp Twist-n-Shout."

Noel smiled coolly at her across their table in Slice of Rome, the lack of concern in his hazel eyes alerting her to the fact that she ought to be acting less interested too.

"I mean, not that it matters," she added with a toss of her recently lightened locks. "We could have hooked up later. Or whatever."

"Yeah," he said, peeling the paper off his straw.

The restaurant was packed that Friday night—everything from families with kids in high chairs to a gang of junior high boys in the corner. There were other couples, too, and a table of four girls Nicole recognized vaguely from CCHS casting envious glances her way. The room was filled with the scents of tomato sauce, pepperoni, and thick, chewy crusts browning in an old-fashioned oven. Nicole's stomach had been growling from the moment they'd walked in, shrinking in despair every time a waitress walked by with a pizza for another table.

"So what do you want to eat?" Noel asked.

"Just a salad," she said reluctantly, bracing for a negative reaction.

"You mean, like, the large antipasto?"

"No, a dinner salad," she corrected, practically holding her breath. Her old boyfriend—if she could even call him that—had constantly nagged her about not eating, as if she were anorexic or something instead of just incredibly disciplined.

Noel, on the other hand, smiled approvingly. "So that's how you stay so thin. It must be tough when everything smells this good."

"It is!" she exclaimed, barely able to believe her luck. Finally, someone who understood! "But it's better than the alternative," she added quickly, one hand straying self-consciously to her flat stomach.

"I hate it when girls let themselves go," he agreed, nodding. "I can't stand fat chicks."

The waitress edged her way through the crowd to take their order. Noel ordered a medium pepperoni pizza for himself, with an order of cheese bread to tide him over while he was waiting.

"Do you want your salad now, or when my pizza comes?" he asked Nicole.

"Better bring it now," Nicole told the waitress, wishing he had at least spared her the appetizer. Slice of Rome's cheese bread was extra good, with three kinds of melting cheese and parsley butter crisping its edges.

Still, I shouldn't complain, she reminded herself quickly. *He's the first person who ever supported my diet. Except for Mom, but that's only because she's so thin herself. Usually.*

Unless Nicole was mistaken, Mrs. Brewster had put on a few pounds in the past couple of months, but no one at home had been foolish enough to mention it. She did that every few years, always finding some crash diet to trim it off again before the situation got out of control.

The waitress left and Noel raked both hands through his dark hair. "I got my hair cut today and I hate it," he complained. "Is it sticking out all goofy?"

"No! It looks great," she assured him.

"Really? I like what you did with yours, too. You bleached it, right?"

"Just a few streaks in the front." She would have loved to go platinum all over, but her mother had said it was subtle or nothing—and she hadn't been in a bargaining mood. "I think this way's more subtle, don't you?"

"Yeah, I like it. It's cool."

"Thanks," she said, basking in the compliment.

"So what are you going to do at cheerleading camp?"

"Oh! It's going to be the best time!" she exclaimed, beginning a step-by-step itinerary for the entire week. The waitress came with the salad and cheese bread somewhere around Day Three, but Nicole left her fork untouched while Noel munched away, glad of a discussion that could take her mind off food. She told him about all the cheers they'd be learning, and about the killer clothes she'd be packing after spending the past three days at the mall with Courtney.

"My mom gave me a bunch of shopping money because it's my seventeenth birthday Thursday," she told him, happy to have found a casual way to work that into the conversation. "At first I wasn't too crazy about having my birthday at camp, but then I started thinking about it and decided it might be cool. It's like having a built-in party, you know?"

Noel grunted, his mouth full of cheese bread.

"Besides, those girls are going to be my best friends next year. Except for Courtney, I mean, because she and I have been best friends forever. And then of course there's—"

Nicole caught herself in midsentence, deciding at the last second against mentioning Eight Prime. Even after all this time Courtney still called them the God Squad, and who knew where Noel stood on the whole God issue? Not Nicole—and she didn't want to, either.

"There's who?" he prompted.

The waitress stopped just long enough to set down a steaming pizza, leaving as quickly as she had arrived.

"Melanie . . . Melanie Andrews," Nicole substituted, figuring she couldn't go wrong naming the most popular girl in school.

"You and Melanie are close?" Noel asked, his eyes widening with interest. Sometimes Nicole wondered if guys even knew how obvious they were.

"Oh, yeah. Me and Melanie are real good friends. Too bad she's not going to be on the cheering squad next year. With me."

Nicole watched as the comment landed. Melanie might be the most beautiful, the most popular, the most *everything* at school, but Nicole finally had a chip of her own to play with. She could practically see Noel picturing her in a green-and-gold cheerleader's uniform, all ready for a game, the center of attention. . . .

"Yeah." He smiled. "Too bad."

She took a bite of her salad, but only to wipe the smug grin off her face. Things were going so well that she wasn't even hungry anymore. She toyed with the last shreds of lettuce while Noel finished up his pizza. Finally he put down the last half-eaten crust and scrubbed his face with a paper napkin.

"Want to go for a drive?" he asked. "Maybe up to the lake?"

Nicole prayed she didn't look as shocked as she felt. Maybe Eight Prime thought the lake was a good place to work their butts off, but to the rest of CCHS, the lake was the makeout spot of choice. If Noel wanted to take her there already, she was really getting somewhere! She thought of Guy Vaughn and how reluctant he had been even to touch her and couldn't believe her good luck. Finally she was with a normal guy. Finally she was with somebody who wanted to be with her!

"I *might* like to drive to the lake," she told Noel. "If . . ."

"If what?" he asked eagerly. He leaned toward her across the table, his jawline tight, his eyes intense. He was so handsome. And of all the girls at school, he'd picked her.

Nicole smiled, satisfied. "*If* you don't have to be home too early."

Five

"I hope Elton knows what he's talking about," Ben muttered, descending the central staircase in Clearwater Crossing's downtown library. It didn't make sense to him that a girl as cute as Bernie Carter would be hanging out in the library on a summer Saturday. Why she would come all the way downtown when there was a satellite branch near her house was even more of a mystery. Ben would have liked to pump Elton for better information, but the last thing he wanted was for anything they'd discussed to get back to Bernie. The whole plan was to convince her he was cool—and turning her seven-year-old brother into a go-between definitely wasn't.

"If she *is* here, where is she hiding?" he wondered under his breath.

He had already checked the teen section and the adult fiction bestsellers. A stroll through the periodicals room had been a waste of time, and she wasn't in Reference, either. Ben was running out of places to look. He was back on the ground floor, loitering by the entrance, when the woman behind the main desk asked if she could help him with something.

"No. I was just, uh . . . I was looking . . . I mean, a friend of mine . . . ," he fumbled, not wanting to tell her what he was up to. Trust no one; give away nothing. Those were the first two rules of being cool.

The librarian nodded knowingly. "If you're looking for Bernie Carter, she's in the computer lab," she said, pointing toward a back corner of the building. "Take the hall past the rest rooms, then make a left."

Ben stared at the woman, stunned. "Bernie Carter?" he repeated, forgetting his own second rule.

"Yeah, wild guess. Am I right?"

"No! I mean . . . that is, I *know* her, but I wasn't *looking* for her. Since she's here, though . . . I mean, I might as well . . ." He slunk off, heart pounding.

Cool, Ben, he reprimanded himself, stopping for a soothing drink of water at the fountain in the hall. He'd sounded like a fool! Still, of all the people in town, how had that woman guessed he was looking for Bernie?

Oh, no, he realized, heart sinking. *She must get guys in here looking for her all the time!*

The thought didn't do much for his confidence. In fact, he seriously considered bolting for the door. Only one thing held him back: the mention of computers.

If Bernie's trying to get something done on a

computer, I could be a big help to her, he thought, seeing a perfect chance to impress.

Mr. Pipkin was a top software engineer at ComAm, and Ben hadn't survived his sixteen years without learning a few tricks from his father. He could troubleshoot just about anything involving hardware, and he was a whiz at basic programming too. Hadn't he helped his dad develop Tomb of Terror, his best-ever 3-D computer game? In fact, if Bernie was into games, maybe he could wow her with a free copy.

Ben started walking again, emboldened. He found the door of the computer lab and slipped inside, only to find himself completely alone with Bernie Carter. Taking a deep breath, he pulled the door closed, then sidled up behind her and peeked at the monitor she was using.

"What is that?" he blurted out, stunned to find the screen full of advanced programming code.

Bernie spun around in the library's swivel chair. "Buh—buh—Ben!" she stammered, startled. "What are you doing here?"

"Are you writing a program?" he asked, ignoring her question.

Bernie's hand shot behind her to clear the screen. "I just, um . . . dabble," she said uneasily. "I don't really know that much about computers."

Ben looked skeptically from the blank screen to her light brown eyes. She could say whatever she wanted; he had seen what he had seen.

"I dabble a bit myself," he said, pulling up a rolling chair. "My dad's a programmer at ComAm. We have computers all over the house."

Bernie's eyes went wide. Impressed. He could tell.

"You know what's weird?" he asked. "The librarian told me to find you in here, like I was looking for you or something. Which I wasn't," he added quickly. "Why would she do that?"

Bernie shrugged. "I have no idea. It's not like I'm always in here. It's just . . . on the weekends . . . I use the computers sometimes, that's all."

"Wouldn't it be easier to use your own?" Ben realized a second too late how rude his question had been. The Carters obviously weren't rich, and the type of programming Bernie was doing required serious hardware.

"I, uh, we don't have an Internet connection at home," she said, her blush making him wonder if she owned a computer at all. "I like to come here and surf a little, pick up my e-mail. That type of thing, you know?"

"What's your e-mail address? Maybe I'll send you something sometime."

"Yeah?" She smiled, showing small white teeth between raspberry-pink-glossed lips. Taking a slip of scratch paper out of the bin beside her, she scribbled her e-mail address with a stubby library pencil: Berniegirl@mailme.com.

"Did somebody already have Bernie?" Ben guessed.

She rolled her eyes; he'd embarrassed her again. "I just wanted people to know," she said. "I mean, that it was me and not some guy."

"Why not just use your full name. What is it? Bernadette?"

"I wish!" The blush on her cheeks deepened until it matched the tiny enameled cherries dangling from her pierced ears. "No, Bernie is my full name. Mom was all set to name *me* Elton, but when I turned out to be a girl, she had to rethink her plan. She was happy with the way things worked out, though. The words come before the music, she says. She says that all the time."

Ben just stared, completely lost.

"It could have been worse, I suppose. The man's lyricist could have been named Harvey, or Poindexter, or something truly awful."

"Are you . . . are you talking about Elton *John?*" Ben asked.

Bernie looked surprised. "I thought . . . well, I just assumed you knew that Elton was named for him. I mean, who else? It's not exactly a common name. Not in Missouri, anyway."

"And you're named for Bernie . . ."

"Taupin," she supplied. "The guy who wrote the words to all those big hits in the seventies. You know, like 'Goodbye Yellow Brick Road' ?"

It sounded vaguely familiar. "I don't know many oldies."

"Don't feel bad. My mother's friends all think me and Elton are such a hoot, but people my age hardly ever make the connection." Bernie sighed. "Maybe that's a good thing."

"At least you're named for someone famous. I'm only named for my father."

"Really? You're Ben junior?"

"Yeah. Kind of embarrassing, huh?"

"I think it's sweet. Me and Elton have different fathers, but I guess you know that."

He hadn't. He thought of asking what had happened to hers, then abruptly decided against it. She'd tell him eventually—if he could keep her talking that long.

"Hey, do you want to get a hot dog?" he asked. "That place across the street is pretty good. I have enough money for us both."

She hesitated, then smiled and stood up, even more slender than he'd remembered. "Okay."

Popping a writable CD out of the computer, she tucked it into her bag and headed for the door. "Are you coming?" she asked over her shoulder.

"Yeah!" Snapping out of his trance, he hurried to open the door for her, then followed her down the hall in a daze.

Had he really just asked Bernie to lunch?

Don't get all excited, he cautioned himself. *You can't call this a date. You didn't even say lunch, you said hot dogs.*

But it was too late—he was already excited. His confidence soared as he walked behind Bernie out the library's front doors.

She's the perfect girl! She's cute and nice—she even likes computers. Not only that, but she honestly seems to believe I'm some sort of cool older guy.

The last thought hit him like a sucker punch as Bernie turned to smile shyly at him from the sidewalk.

How can I ever maintain such a completely unfounded illusion?

"I have to talk to you about something," Miguel told his mother after lunch. He must have sounded more intense than he'd intended, because she froze with their dishes halfway to the sink.

"Is everything okay?"

"Yes, fine. I didn't mean to make a big deal."

Jumping up, he took the sandwich plates away from her and set them on the counter. "Sit back down, all right?"

His younger sister, Rosa, was at a friend's that Saturday afternoon, and if Miguel was ever going to tell his mother about his scheme to get the family their own house, now seemed like the perfect time. He had kept the plan to himself as long as he could, turning it over and over in his mind until he was positive it was perfect, but he couldn't take the next step without his mother's approval—not to mention her active involvement.

"What's going on, *mi vida?*" she asked, still apprehensive as she reclaimed her seat at the dinette. "What is this about?"

Miguel sank into the vinyl chair across from hers. "You know how we're saving to move out of this dump and into a bigger apartment?"

A shadow crossed her face. "It's not a dump, Miguel. A dump would be dirty, and this place is spotless."

"All right. I know." He hated living in public housing, but it was no time to argue semantics. "We're saving to move out of here anyway, right?"

"Now that I'm well, we can stand on our own feet again. We don't need any more assistance," she said with a flash of the pride he'd inherited.

"Exactly. And what if I told you that instead of renting an apartment, I know a way we can buy a house? A *big* house, all our own."

His mother searched his face as if trying to find the joke. Her brown eyes seemed tired, but her graying hair was as neat as ever, wound into a perfect knot in back. "I guess I'd have to ask what you've been smoking," she said at last.

Miguel rolled his eyes impatiently. His mom would have a heart attack if she ever really believed he was using drugs.

"No, Mom. I'm serious."

"How could we afford a house, *mi amor?* You know we only have a couple thousand dollars in savings, barely enough to cover a new apartment and moving fees. Houses are much more expensive—to buy *and* to own. When things break, you have to pay to fix them. It's not like an apartment, where you can make the landlord deal with it."

"I know. I remember," he said testily.

"No, Miguel. You were much younger when we had the house. And your father was alive then, to make the payments and take care of things. And anyway, this whole discussion is pointless because we just don't have the money. I'm sorry, baby. A house is out of the question."

"I'm going to be eighteen pretty soon. And I'm not as dumb as you think."

She rocked back in her chair, shocked. "Miguel! I don't think you're—"

"Then just let me *tell* you! All right?"

"All right." She composed herself, folding her hands on the table, while Miguel took a few deep breaths.

"That old guy, Charlie Johnson, the one whose house Jesse and I painted? He says he wants to sell out and move to a nursing home. He only lives a few streets over. You know which house it is?"

"I think so. I'm not certain."

"Well, it's two stories. Big. And it needs a little work—all right, a lot of work—but I could fix it, Mom. I could. And since I'll be going to college at

CU, I'll be home for a few more years, at least. I think you ought to come look at it."

"Oh, Miguel," she said with a sigh. "Even if I wanted you to spend more time working than you already do, where would we get the down payment?"

"But that's the best part!" Quickly, before she could close her mind again, he explained that Charlie was willing to carry the loan for the house himself, so that they'd be making payments to him instead of a bank. "He doesn't need the money up front. I guess he'd rather have the interest."

Mrs. del Rios didn't look convinced.

"I'll work, Mom. I *want* to work," Miguel added before she could object. "And you're doing all right at the department store now. . . ."

His mother closed her eyes, obviously bracing to disappoint him.

"Think what it would mean to Rosa!" he pleaded. "To be back in a regular house again, to be normal, like her friends. It's a good house, Mom, and I'll make it better. If you wanted to, you could live there the rest of your life."

"Oh, Miguel." She sighed again. "I don't even know what to say."

"Say you'll look at it," he urged.

Peter collapsed onto the wrought-iron bench in front of his church, exhausted. "I may never move again," he told Jenna as she plopped down beside him. "I may just sit here right through to next Sunday."

She laughed, and he was glad to hear how much better she sounded. Her cold had cleared up enough to allow her to talk normally, and her chapped nose had faded from red to pink. She hadn't sung in the choir that morning, still too clogged to hit the high notes, but she was definitely well enough to come back to camp.

And not a moment too soon, he thought, remembering the hour-by-hour traumas of the week before and the scrambling he'd done just to keep the activities covered.

"I'm exhausted," he said. The only thing keeping him going was the knowledge that Monday was Memorial Day, which meant only a four-day week for camp.

"Why don't we go on a picnic?" she suggested. "I'll make us some sandwiches and we can ride our bikes to—"

"Jenna?"

"Yes?"

"No offense, but I never want to eat outdoors again. Besides, my dad wants me to help him pour that concrete patio out back today. We'll be at it all afternoon and probably most of the holiday, too."

"That's awful! Can't you just tell him you're too tired?"

Peter shrugged. "It won't be that bad. No one crying, or whining, or shooting foul things at me through a straw . . . In fact, I might even enjoy it."

"At least with Memorial Day, camp will be a day shorter next week," she said, reading his mind.

"We'll still be missing Nicole, though, and it seems like Miguel's schedule changes daily. Can a hospital really be that disorganized, or do you think he's jerking me around?"

He had meant it to be a rhetorical question, but something strange entered Jenna's blue eyes. "What is he doing exactly?" she asked. "I mean, is he coming late, leaving early? What?"

She was obviously hanging on his answer, which made him suddenly nervous. Anyone who knew Jenna could tell she had cards she wasn't showing.

"Nothing like that," he said uneasily. "He just never wants to commit to anything in advance."

"Doesn't want to commit!" she snorted with heavy irony. "I know what you mean!"

"You do?"

"Have you noticed anything else about him lately?" Jenna prodded.

"Like what?"

"Like the way he treats Leah, maybe?"

Peter shook his head, baffled. "As far as I can tell, he treats her the same as always."

"It looks that way, doesn't it?" Her voice lowered to a whisper. "I can't stand it anymore—I have to tell you this. The other day I was driving through his neighborhood and I saw—"

"Jenna!" Maggie interrupted, sneaking up and grabbing the back of the bench. The wrought iron jiggled in her hands, jarring Peter's aching head. "We're leaving now. Come on."

"All right. I'll be there in a minute."

"Dad said get you *now*." Maggie's hands left the bench and dropped to her hips as she prepared to stare Jenna down. Her freckles were as prominent as ever, but Peter noticed she was wearing her auburn hair differently, in a tightly smoothed roll that seemed intended to hide its curliness. A few springy strands had escaped nonetheless, making corkscrews around her face.

"I'll be there in a *minute*," Jenna repeated stubbornly. "I'm talking to Peter about something."

Maggie crossed her arms and tapped her foot, obviously intending to stand there and wait. Jenna's lips pressed into a line; she clearly had no intention of continuing their conversation in front of Maggie. And Peter suddenly realized he was glad of the stalemate. Whatever Jenna was trying to tell him about Miguel, he really didn't want to know.

"Maybe you ought to go," he told her, earning a triumphant look from Maggie. "You don't want to keep your family waiting."

Jenna sighed heavily. "I guess I can call you tonight."

"Yeah, do that. But Jenna? I don't want to talk about Miguel, all right? I mean, not unless it has something to do with you, me, or camp."

She opened her mouth to argue, then shut it again and shrugged. Whatever was on her mind was obviously still bothering her as she walked away, but he hoped she'd forget it quickly.

If she needs me for something, that's different. But if all she wants is to gossip . . .

As much as he loved Jenna, he didn't like getting involved in other people's business nearly as much as she did.

Six

"Are you sure you have everything?" Mrs. Brewster asked, looking over the bags she and Nicole had set down in the school parking lot. It was just after noon on Monday, and CCHS's new cheerleading squad was loading up to leave for Camp Twist-n-Shout.

"I'm fine. You can go now," Nicole returned through a tightly clenched smile. "I'll call you to pick me up when we get back Friday night."

"If I didn't know better, I'd think you were trying to get rid of me," Mrs. Brewster said, raising penciled brows. "But a big girl like you is too mature to be ashamed of being seen with her mommy."

"Mom, please," Nicole begged under her breath. "Do you see any other parents here?"

Not thirty feet away, Sandra Kincaid, the cheerleading coach, was half hidden between the double back doors of a rented white van. Tanya, Angela, and Kara were handing her backpacks, bags, and suitcases from a massive pile, while Debbie, Lou Anne, and Sidney seemed to have already claimed the rearmost bench seat inside. As Nicole watched, a truck pulled up next to the van and Becca and Maria tumbled out, unloading their stuff while their twenty-something driver waited with the engine running.

"At least you can stop worrying about bringing too much stuff," Mrs. Brewster said. "I've never seen so much luggage for just ten girls."

"And a coach," Nicole added defensively.

But to herself she admitted her mother was right. When Nicole had gone to the U.S. Girls modeling contest in Los Angeles with the other girls from Eight Prime, she'd been the one with the most stuff by far. Now, looking down at the four bags around her feet, she felt positively restrained. She was finally traveling with her own kind of people!

"I still can't believe you're leaving on Memorial Day," Mrs. Brewster complained. "Especially since camp doesn't even start until tomorrow."

"It's not like our family ever does anything for Memorial Day anyway. I mean, eat a burger for me or something. But the squad has to check into the dorms and rest up tonight so we'll be ready to start bright and early tomorrow."

"I don't know why they had to choose a camp all the way in St. Louis."

"Mom, please! You're killing me. Could you just let me go now?"

"All right." Mrs. Brewster heaved a sigh and bent

to kiss Nicole on the forehead. "My little baby grew up so fast. I can't believe you're already sixteen!"

"Seventeen," Nicole corrected automatically. "Practically."

Mrs. Brewster finally climbed into her Mustang and drove away, Nicole waving her off with relief. She couldn't have said exactly what was different about her mother lately, but there was no denying she'd been acting strange. All nostalgic and mushy and . . . ick.

Nicole shuddered as she picked up her bags. *Not like herself at all.*

"Hey, Nicole!" Tanya Jeffries, their squad leader, called. "Come on! Let's load up and get out of here!"

"Sounds good to me!" Nicole called back, smiling as she trotted to the rapidly filling van.

It took quite a while to stuff everything in. Then Jamila Kane showed up and the process began anew. There were so many bags that Nicole kept one of hers out to hold in her lap. Sandra finally forced the double back doors shut, and everyone piled into the van.

As captain, Tanya claimed the prized shotgun position in the bucket seat next to Sandra's, and since the backseat was already full, the remaining six girls split up between the first and second benches. Nicole scored a great spot in the center of the first bench, sandwiched between Becca and Kara.

"Turn on the radio!" Debbie called as their coach

pulled out of the parking lot to start the two-hour drive to St. Louis.

"In a minute," Sandra replied. "First I have a few things to say about camp."

Everyone quieted down to give the coach their full attention.

"Tanya has the list of room assignments, which she'll be passing around in a minute," Sandra informed them. "Bear in mind that we're a team and supposed to get along, so I don't want to hear any complaining about who's rooming with who."

Nicole kept the smile on her face, but she couldn't deny an anxious twinge. She hadn't gotten off to the best possible start with the squad, and even though things had recently taken a turn for the better, she still had no illusions about being its most popular member. In fact, there were at least a couple of girls who pretty actively disliked her.

What if my roommate is Debbie or Lou Anne? For that matter, I'm not too sure about Jamila, either. Please, God, let it be Tanya, or Angela, or Kara. . . .

"When we get to camp," Sandra went on, "I don't want any fooling around in the parking lot or in Wagner Hall, where we'll sign in and pick up our room keys. Everyone gets their stuff, gets their key, and goes straight to their room to unpack. Got it?"

She glanced in the rearview mirror to make sure everyone was still paying attention. "I'm not against having fun—and we will. But don't ever forget that we're there representing our school. The way we comport ourselves reflects on all of CCHS. Not to mention that if we have any problems this first time out, we won't get to go back."

Debbie raised her hand. "We're not going to stay in our rooms all night?" she asked in a horrified tone.

"Of course not," Sandra said. "I just want to be one hundred percent sure that everyone is settled in and ready to give camp their all. Then we'll go to the dinner mixer with the other teams that come in tonight."

"Pass back those room assignments, Tanya," Lou Anne ordered from the backseat.

"Yes, thank you, Lou Anne," Sandra said sarcastically. "As a matter of fact, I *was* finished speaking." She shook her head and flipped on the radio.

Tanya passed the room assignments to the first row, where Nicole discovered—to her immense relief—that she had been paired with Kara Tibbs. Kara might not be the coolest or most popular girl on the squad, but Nicole had already come to appreciate her pleasant, accepting nature.

"It looks like we're going to be roomies," Kara said as the assignment sheet continued its rounds. "I hope we get a good room."

"We're going to have an awesome time," Nicole promised. "I brought everything: magazines, and all my makeup, and more clothes than I can possibly wear. Maybe we can swap—I think we're about the same size."

"I wish!" said Kara, rolling her gray eyes.

"I'll bet we are," Nicole insisted. Kara was shorter than she was, but that wouldn't matter except in long pants. "Oh! And I brought a ton of CDs and my curling iron and crimper. You can use them if you want."

"Thanks."

Kara seemed favorably impressed, but Nicole wanted her to be blown away. Her goal was to have the largest possible number of squad members loving her by the end of the week, and Kara was definitely the easiest place to start. She racked her brain for more ways to earn points as the other girls all talked at the same time, making plans with their new roommates.

"Oh!" Nicole added, digging through the tote on her lap. "And I hope you like chocolate, because I brought a lot of it."

She found a one-pound bag of M&M's, opened it, and offered the whole thing to Kara. "Go ahead. Help yourself."

"Aren't you having any?" Kara asked a little suspiciously.

"Oh. Um, sure." Reluctantly Nicole helped herself to a small handful—anything to fit in. "Take all you want and pass the rest back. There's plenty more where that came from."

Plenty more, she repeated silently. Having an endless supply of free sugar to share was part of her squad-pleasing strategy.

"Pass that candy back here," Sidney said.

"Yeah, quit hogging all the chocolate," Lou Anne demanded.

"It's okay. I have more," Nicole said loudly, wanting everyone to know where the candy had come from.

Debbie snorted. "You know what they say," she told Lou Anne, in a voice meant to be overheard. "Some girls have dates, and the rest drown their sorrows in sugar."

"Is that what they say?" asked Nicole, surprising herself with her own nonchalance. "I'll have to tell that to Noel Phillips the next time we go out." Looking directly at Debbie, Nicole put the whole fistful of M&M's in her mouth and chewed with pretended gusto.

"Noel Phillips?" Becca squealed. "That guy is totally cute!"

"Yeah. Not bad." Nicole could barely believe her own ears. It seemed an alien had taken over her body—a cool, quick-thinking alien who didn't take any guff from Debbie. Nicole smiled; she liked being from that planet.

"Come on," Lou Anne scoffed, obviously not convinced. "When did you go out with Noel?"

"Friday. He asked for my number at a grad night party, but I've been pretty busy since then."

"Yeah, right," Debbie said sarcastically. "*You* had a hot date with Noel Phillips. Where'd he take you? Out to pizza?"

"As a matter of fact, he did."

Debbie rolled her eyes, telling the entire van how unromantic she thought that was.

"Right before we drove up to the lake," Nicole added.

"Ooooh, *Nicole*!"

"No way!"

"To the *lake*?"

Everyone but Debbie believed her now. The van was full of screams of congratulations.

"How does he kiss?" Becca asked, wide-eyed. "We won't tell anyone."

"Was he good?" Sidney demanded.

Actually, he had only kissed her twice, and he had tasted of pepperoni. Still, Nicole had been more than willing to overlook that then, and she didn't think she should mention it now.

"I'll never tell," she said instead, smiling mysteriously.

"Are you going to see him again?" Kara asked.

Nicole didn't let the fact that they had no plans whatsoever faze her. "If I feel like it," she said, reaching for more M&M's.

Her bored tone set everyone laughing, and soon the van was full of romantic confessions: guys they had dated, guys they were dying to get their hands on, guys they wouldn't touch with a ten-foot pole. Nicole smiled as the melting chocolate slid down her throat, making her victory that much sweeter.

I am so in! she thought happily. *They like me and we aren't even there yet!*

Maybe this isn't such a good idea, Jenna thought nervously, watching Miguel park his beat-up old car at the curb in front of his house. *Maybe I should just go home and mind my own business, like Peter said.*

She shook her head. *Okay, he didn't say that* exactly. *But I know that's what he meant.*

Instead she had borrowed her mother's car and parked on the del Rioses' street, waiting and worrying. It certainly wasn't as if she was looking *forward* to telling Miguel she had seen him with Sabrina—she just didn't know what else to do. All week long the knowledge of his infidelity had been like an insect bite she'd scratched and scratched until it had become an open wound. She had worried and stewed and prayed until she was half crazy. Just knowing about it was bad enough, but having to keep it to herself . . .

That part's killing me.

Jenna had tried to be honest with herself, and she didn't think she was just being nosy, either. She certainly hadn't *asked* to know what Miguel was doing behind Leah's back. But once a person knew something like that, wasn't it her duty to do something about it? Wouldn't turning her back on the situation be worse than anything she could say?

Jenna's hand closed around the car door handle before she could lose her nerve. "Miguel!" she called, stepping into the street.

He seemed amazed to see her as she joined him on the sidewalk, probably because she wasn't in the habit of stopping by his house.

"I need to talk to you," she blurted out.

"Sure," he said, glancing toward his house. "You want to come in?"

A blue hospital smock was draped over his arm, a clue that he'd just come from work. Unless he had progressed in his cheating to the point where he'd started using disguises . . .

Jenna felt sick as she looked up into the clear brown eyes that had once seemed so perfectly honest. "I saw you kissing Sabrina," she said. "I know all about it, and I'm going to tell Leah."

The blood drained from his face. His hands opened and closed as if looking for something to hang on to. "I can't . . . I mean . . . that wasn't what it looked like," he said. "You have to let me explain."

Jenna crossed her arms over her chest. She had come to hear an explanation, but it was hard to imagine one that could change her mind.

"Can we . . . ? Let's just sit down, all right?" His hand shook as he opened his car door to offer her the passenger seat, but Jenna refused to let that sway her.

He ought to be afraid, she thought unsympathetically as he walked around to the driver's side. *He ought to be* very *afraid*.

"Okay?" Miguel asked nervously, settling into his seat. "Is this all right?"

Jenna arms remained stubbornly crossed. "I'm listening."

"The thing is," Miguel said, his eyes begging her to believe him, "I *didn't* kiss Sabrina."

"Oh, please!" she exclaimed, rising halfway out of her seat. "I was driving down the street and I saw you with my own—"

"I know what you must have seen," he said quickly. His hand caught her by the forearm, keeping her in the car. "I know *exactly* what you must have seen, because it only happened once. See, I took Sabrina over to have a look at Charlie's house, and on the way back we stopped to talk in the shade. Talking was all *I* had in mind, but the next thing I knew, Sabrina was attached to my lips. I swear I had nothing to do with it."

"Nothing to do with it!" Jenna repeated with a snort. "I *saw* you, Miguel! You weren't exactly roped and tied."

She expected him to argue, but instead he released her arm and buried his face in his hands.

"You're right. I am such an idiot," he moaned. "I completely deserve this. Leah warned me and warned me—and I knew, to be perfectly honest. I knew Sabrina had some sort of thing for me. But I honestly thought I was in control the situation." He looked up again, tears sparkling in his black lashes. "I mean, I'm a *guy*, for crying out loud. If I say I'm not interested, shouldn't that be enough?"

Jenna simply stared, too speechless at this sudden turn to argue gender politics.

"And I *knew* I ought to tell Leah," Miguel went on, "but you must have some idea how mad she's going to be. Instead I told Sabrina she could forget it, so that friendship is over. *Completely* over," he repeated, as if to make sure Jenna was listening. "I guess . . . I guess I convinced myself I got away with it. Not that I got away with anything!" he added quickly, obviously realizing how bad that had sounded. "I mean . . . I just thought . . ." He sighed. "I was a total coward."

"Well, I—I—" Jenna stammered, at a loss for words.

"You still think you need to tell Leah." His eyes bored into hers, resigned yet intense. "But be fair, Jenna. Tell her the whole story. Better yet, let me tell her."

"*You* want to tell her?"

"I'd give anything! Will you . . . will you let me?"

Jenna felt a huge weight fly off of her shoulders. She took a long, clean breath, her whole body seeming to float upward with the inhalation.

"Yes," she said, unable to disguise her relief. "I

mean, just so long as someone does," she added gruffly. She didn't want Miguel to think he was totally off the hook.

But gruff clearly wasn't her best expression, because the next thing she knew Miguel had folded her into a hard bear hug.

"You're a good friend, Jenna," he said. "To Leah *and* to me. Thank God you didn't just go and tell her behind my back! Can you imagine?"

Yeah, Jenna thought, smiling as she remembered the number of times she had prayed about what to do. *Thank you, God.*

If she *had* gone directly to Leah, if she *had* told her friend that her boyfriend was cheating . . .

Thanks for getting me out of this mess!

"How many of those are you going to eat?" Melanie asked, more amazed than disgusted.

Jesse lifted his fifth hot dog off the rusty public grill and tucked it into a waiting bun. "Well, they come eight to a package, and if you're only going to eat one . . . You do the math," he told her, taking a big bite.

Melanie pressed both hands to her belly, imagining the ache. She had finished her own perfectly filling hot dog long before. Now she reclined on a blanket in the gathering dusk at Clearwater Crossing Park, watching the fireflies rise from the grass. Roasting hot dogs in the park had been Jesse's impromptu Memorial Day idea. At first she had been concerned about someone from school spotting them together, but it was late enough, and the crowd had thinned out enough, that she had totally relaxed.

"You could at least sit down," she invited, patting the blanket next to her. "Your feet could probably use the break, what with that extra load you're putting on them."

He rolled his eyes and took one last bite, tossing the leftover scrap of bun into the trash can next to the grill.

"You're not funny," he said, dropping down beside her. "And I was full anyway."

"No kidding, Oinky," she said, pushing him playfully. "Keep it up and next year you'll be blocking instead of running."

She was kidding, of course. He looked fantastic and they both knew it. In fact, lately, when they were alone together, she had to practically force herself not to think about his body. Regardless of the mistakes she had made with guys in the past—and she'd made some whoppers—she had no intention of going down the same road with Jesse. And whatever his past experiences with girls had been—and she was certain he'd had some—he was just going to have to respect that. She wasn't rushing into anything ever again. This time everything would be slow, and careful, and right. . . .

"I think you're getting a little extra around the

middle too," he teased, grabbing for her ribs. His hands on her skin were an electric jolt, and not because he was tickling.

"Stop it!" she squealed, rolling away.

But Jesse anticipated her move, rolling alongside her. They tumbled off the blanket and into the grass, his body ending on top of hers. Melanie could feel the moisture seeping through the back of her cropped blouse, but that sensation barely registered compared to the heat of him on her belly. Nothing existed for her in that moment except Jesse, and the beating of their two hearts, and the way his eyes searched her face. There was something about his expression, something so close to love . . .

She closed her eyes and kissed him, afraid where that look might lead. They were together, and that was enough. Maybe they weren't officially boyfriend and girlfriend, the way Jesse wanted them to be. Maybe the details weren't worked out yet. All Melanie knew was that she could barely breathe when he wasn't around, could barely close her eyes unless her head was resting against his shoulder. She didn't need to hear him say he loved her, too.

At least not while there was any chance he might take it back.

Soon, she told herself, breathing in the smell of his skin, his hair. *Soon, but not yet.*

Seven

"Go, Wildcats!" Nicole screamed at the top of her lungs. "Go! Fight! Win!" Her voice was so loud it could have filled the enormous university gym, but she could barely hear herself as her entire squad screamed with her in perfect unison.

"Go, Hornets!" came the thundering reply. "Go, fight, win!"

"Go, Lightning!" rebounded from the end of the gym.

"Go, Gators!"

"Go, Bounders!"

"Go! Fight! Win!"

The Twist-n-Shout camp director raised the spirit stick higher above her head. She was standing on a stepladder in the center of the gym so that all the squads packed onto the floor could see her. The higher the spirit stick went, the louder the teams were supposed to yell. As far as Nicole could tell, the stick couldn't get any higher—or the cheers any louder.

The cheerleaders screamed through their rotations

again, each team striving to achieve its full ear-splitting potential. All morning long they'd been working on the camp segment called "Chants, Yells, and Projection," learning new rhymes and practicing their unison. When the Wildcats' final turn came, Nicole yelled with so much fervor, it felt like she ripped something loose in her throat. Then all the squads started cheering spontaneously to show the full extent of their spirit. The director lowered the stick and held up an empty hand; the gym fell abruptly silent.

"Excellent!" she said, beaming. "We've made excellent progress this morning. This is the finest group of squads I think we've ever seen."

Cheers broke out again.

"I'll bet she says that at every camp," Tanya muttered, but Nicole could tell she was pleased anyway.

"We'll break for lunch now," the director announced, "after which we'll meet on the playing fields for 'Dance and Choreography.' Coaches, please lead your squads from the gym in an orderly fashion."

Girls stampeded for the doors, eager to be first in the cafeteria. Nicole felt her stomach rumble but held her ground, knowing Sandra would make them eat last if they tried to push their way forward.

"So much for leaving in an orderly fashion," Sidney grumbled, casting a hopeful sideways look at Sandra.

Their coach simply waited for the path to the

door to clear, leaving the squad no choice but to wait beside her. There might be power struggles between individual girls, but no one disputed who was in charge when Sandra was around.

At last they made their way outside, crossing steaming grass and simmering asphalt before reaching the air-conditioned cafeteria. Nicole fell into line behind Kara, wishing once again that Sandra had consulted the squad about the practice uniforms she had surprised them with the night before. The T-shirts were boxy and white, featureless except for the gold CCHS across the chest, and the green shorts they tucked into were far from sexy. It was kind of exciting to be dressed alike, especially since the other squads were too, but when Nicole thought of all the much cuter outfits languishing in her dorm room . . .

"I'm going to drink about a gallon of iced tea," Kara announced, pushing sweaty strings of mouse-brown hair off her face. "My throat is so dry from all that yelling."

"I think I ripped something in mine," Nicole said hoarsely, massaging the sore spot.

"Have some of that self-serve frozen yogurt," Becca volunteered from behind her. "I had it last night, and it's really good, especially with all those syrups and sprinkles they have to choose from. Something cold ought to make you feel better."

Nicole's stomach rumbled again. Breakfast for

most of the girls that morning had been cereal, past-ries, sausages, eggs, and fruit, but all Nicole had eaten was a banana. Now, as she neared the food ser-vice area, the smells of burgers and fries floated to her like exotic perfume. Their aromas, combined with the thought of a cool, creamy bowl of frozen yogurt, played havoc with her willpower.

You wouldn't be so hungry if you hadn't completely pigged out yesterday, she scolded herself, remember-ing all the chocolate she'd eaten in the van and the huge slice of greasy pizza she'd had for dinner. There wasn't a scale in her dorm room, but she had to have done some damage. That morning she'd been deter-mined to go right back on her diet, but they'd been up so early, and exercising so much . . .

"I'll have a hamburger and fries," she heard herself telling the white-coated woman behind the lunch counter.

"Me too," Kara said.

Becca ordered the same, and the three of them headed straight to the frozen yogurt dispenser.

In the enormous dining area, everyone was segre-gated by squad. The whole room was divided into patchwork blocks of red, or blue, or green T-shirts. The three girls found a table with the rest of their team and began eating as if starved.

"This is so *good*!" Maria said to answering grunts.

Nicole had a huge bite of hamburger in her

mouth, but she shoved a piping hot fry in as well, carried away by the feeding frenzy all around her.

"Your yogurt's going to melt," Debbie told her snottily. "You should have gotten that afterward."

"Yeah, if there's any left," said Becca. "They ran out last night."

Debbie looked a bit alarmed.

"Anyway, melting's not a problem," said Nicole, rubbing it in. "There's no rule says I have to eat dessert last."

She took a big bite of the frozen yogurt, letting it slide soothingly down her raw throat. It felt amazingly good—cool and chocolaty. For a moment she even imagined herself going back for a second helping.

Then she looked down at the loaded tray in front of her and felt the first twinge of panic. She couldn't believe she was even considering eating what was already there, let alone going back for more.

You have enough. Too much, she told herself. *Only eat half.*

It was good advice, but it was hard to take with everyone chowing down around her. The other girls on the squad were all reasonably thin, and Nicole didn't see anyone else starving herself. She took a second, more modest bite of yogurt, then followed it up with a spoonful so huge she could barely get it all into her mouth.

What the heck, she thought, giving in. *I'll work it off this afternoon.*

"What movie are we seeing, again?" Leah asked Miguel, turning onto the backcountry road that ended at the drive-in.

Miguel looked up from his lap. "Huh? I thought *you* knew."

"It was your idea to come here." She knew she'd never be able to concentrate on a movie with her guilty conscience.

"I thought I just said we could come if you wanted, and you said yes."

"Did I?" She couldn't remember. "We're getting to be like an old married couple."

Miguel gave her a weak smile as she drove up to the entrance. They paid their admission, then pulled into a space and set up the speaker.

"Do you want the top down?" Leah asked.

"If you do," he said with a shrug.

She was reaching for the control when his hand reached out to stop her. "Maybe we should leave it up a minute. We need to talk about something."

A chill ran through her. There was no reason to assume he meant something bad, but intuition told her he did. Had he somehow found out about Shane?

She turned nervously to face him, the surrounding cars and the still-blank screen at the front of the drive-in completely forgotten. Miguel shifted back

98

and forth, looking as uncomfortable as she felt. His eyes darted from the dashboard to the gearshift to his thumbnail—anywhere but at her.

This is going to be bad, she thought with a creeping feeling of dread. *I have no idea how he found out, but he definitely knows.*

"Before you say anything, I just want to tell you it was all a huge mistake," she blurted out. "I have no intention of ever seeing Shane again."

He stared at her, dumbfounded. "What?"

"That, uh . . . that wasn't what you wanted to talk about?" she asked with a sinking feeling.

"Who's Shane?"

Her breath caught in her chest. She should have told him. But not like this.

"Nobody, really. What did *you* want to talk about?"

"You're seeing another guy?" he asked disbelievingly.

"No! No, don't even think that! It was just a mistake, that's all."

"Did you go out with this Shane?"

"No! Well, yes. But not really." The next minute she was pouring out the entire story, how she'd met Shane, how he had pursued her, how she had resisted. Mostly. Her courage almost failed her as she told Miguel about being in Shane's arms, on the verge of that fateful kiss, but she got it all out somehow. By the time she finished, Miguel's eyes had grown coldly furious.

"That son of a—"

"But I didn't actually kiss him!" she repeated tearfully. "I swear, Miguel, I don't even know why I went there. I don't love anyone but you. I *love* you," she repeated, her whole heart in the words.

She tried to take his hand, but he shook her off, making her cry even harder. "I know . . . that's no excuse," she sobbed, covering her face. "You would never do a thing like that to me. . . ."

For a long time the only sound in the car was Leah's brokenhearted crying. She found herself thankful they had left the top up so that no one else could hear her, but it was getting hot with the AC off. Part of her wondered if this was what hell would be like, stifling heat and a person's own guilt choking her for eternity . . .

Then Miguel put a hand on her shoulder.

"I'm not mad at you," he said. "But if I ever meet that sleazeball Shane . . ." She felt a shudder pass through his body. "Anyway, I'm just as bad as you are. Worse. See, me and Sabrina—"

Leah went rigid, horrified to hear that name in the context of the current conversation. Her eyes snapped up to his.

"I mean, Sabrina and I . . ."

He thought she was reacting to his *grammar*?

". . . um, anyway, we went over to take a look at the outside of Charlie's house and . . . um . . . don't freak out, but she kind of . . . kissed me."

"She *what?*"

"It just happened, I swear! We were talking on the sidewalk and—"

"Sabrina Ambrosi *kissed* you? And you were sitting there letting *me* feel guilty? How *could* you?"

She was fumbling with the door handle, desperate to get away from him, when she suddenly remembered whose car they were in.

"Get out!" she demanded, pushing against his chest with both hands. "Get out of my car this minute!"

"Aw, Leah. You don't mean that."

For about two seconds she stared him down, searching for just the right words to cut him to the quick. Then she burst into tears. The next thing she knew, she was in his arms, sobbing into his shirt, and he was apologizing into her hair, over and over, until she gradually believed there was nothing romantic between him and Sabrina—and remembered that she wasn't entirely blameless herself.

"How could we let this happen?" she asked at last, wiping her eyes with the backs of her hands. "We knew what they were like."

Miguel shook his head. "I don't know. But it won't happen twice. I told Sabrina to stay away from me. And I hope . . ."

"I'm not going to see Shane," Leah finished for him. "I haven't even talked to him since I went running out of his dorm."

"Then it's over," he said. "It's over, right? I mean, this doesn't change anything between us."

"No," Leah agreed, letting her arms slip down his body so that she could sink back into her seat. "Not between us."

He still looked worried. "Are you mad at me?"

"Not really."

"Not *really*?"

"A little," she admitted. "I'll get over it."

"Because I could be mad at you, too, you know."

"Are you?"

He shrugged. "I'll get over it."

"I just wish . . . I wish Sabrina didn't live in Clearwater Crossing," Leah said. "She's been after you since day one. How do we know she's given up?"

"What about Shane?" Miguel countered. "I wish that guy didn't even live in Missouri!"

Leah smiled weakly, ignoring the sick sensation in her gut. She knew she ought to mention that Shane wouldn't be in Missouri much longer, because he'd be moving to California to go to Stanford, same as she would. But she couldn't. Not right then.

I'll definitely tell him later, she thought. *I'll tell him, and then this entire thing will truly be behind us.*

I hope, she added uneasily.

Sabrina had shown amazing persistence with regard to Miguel, and Shane wasn't exactly good at taking no for an answer either. What if he *did* call her again? Or what if Miguel did more work for Mr. Ambrosi and ended up on another crew with Sabrina?

"I'm not going to see Shane. And you're not going to see Sabrina, so let's just try to forget about it," she said.

"All right," he agreed. "We'll forget it."

But long after the movie had started, even after they'd put the top down on the convertible and opened their seats to the stars, Leah knew they hadn't forgotten.

Neither of them was thinking of anything else.

Eight

"Chris!" Melanie exclaimed, surprised to see him walking a group of campers into the cabin. Chris hadn't been to camp since the first Monday, tied up as he was with summer classes at college and a part-time job. He hadn't even been there earlier that same Wednesday. "What are you doing here? And how come you have Peter's group?"

"I felt like dropping by," Chris said as the boys he'd brought in for crafts scrambled to get the best chairs. "I'm not working today, and the class I'm supposed to be in . . ." He shrugged, a mischievous smile on his lips. "Call this a mental health day."

"Move over!" Jason ordered loudly, trying to shove Danny out of a chair in the front row. "I was here first."

"Oh, yeah? Then how come my butt's already in the seat?" Danny challenged, pushing back. One of his legs wrapped around the chair; the other stretched behind him, scrabbling for traction on the smooth plywood floor.

"You call *this* mental health?" Melanie asked Chris dubiously. "Maybe I'll just skip college."

Chris stepped forward to separate the scuffling boys.

"You guys'll spill the paint," Louis warned, reaching for the nearest cup. His hand knocked it over just as Chris leaned across the table, sending a violent splash of red across Chris's shirt and shorts.

Everyone froze to see what Chris would do, but he just stood there, staring down at his clothes in disbelief.

"Good one, Louis," Jason finally muttered.

Chris gave him a look that shut him up immediately. Melanie tried to hand Chris some paper towels.

"Thanks, but I think my only chance to get this mess out is a long swim underwater. Can you keep an eye on these guys?"

"I, uh . . . I guess," she said uncertainly. The only reason she was even in crafts that day was because Jenna had wanted to be outside for a change. On top of that, Melanie had never been in charge of a boys' group before—not to mention that Peter usually took the biggest troublemakers for himself.

"Where *is* Peter?" she asked Louis as Chris disappeared out the door.

The little boy shrugged. "He said he had to make another new schedule."

Melanie threw her paper towels down to cover the small amount of paint that had missed Chris and landed on the table.

"I don't want any trouble from you guys," she warned, passing out sheets of card stock that had been donated by a local copy shop. "This is good paper, so just settle down and paint something nice to take home." Out of the corner of her eye, she saw Jason brandishing a loaded yellow paintbrush at her. "Or I'll tell Peter and Chris and you can sit out during swimming today," she added.

"Beaching" was the only real threat the counselors could make, but, as usual, it worked. Melanie heaved a sigh of relief as Jason lowered the brush to his paper and all the boys began painting. They were completely absorbed in their creations by the time Chris reappeared at the doorway, his hair and shorts still dripping and his T-shirt twisted into a rope he wrung out over the dirt.

"I think I got it all out," he told her. "I hope I didn't kill any fish."

"That stuff is totally nontoxic," she reassured him, trying not to be flustered by the fact that she had never seen him without his shirt on before. She had found Chris good-looking ever since the first time she'd laid eyes on him in Clearwater Crossing Park. "The package says you're supposed to be able to eat it."

"Nobody get any ideas!" Chris said quickly, stepping inside far enough to shoot his group a meaningful look.

"What?" a couple of them said innocently. Everyone kept painting.

Chris turned as he retreated back onto the doorstep, and Melanie got her first look at the tattoo on his right arm. She had known he had one—she had noticed the bottom edge of it peeking from his shirt sleeve—but she'd never seen enough of it before to figure out what it was.

"You . . . you have a cross," she said, astonished.

"Huh?" He followed her eyes, glancing down over his right shoulder. "Oh. Yeah. You never saw that?"

"I just . . . well . . . no."

She'd heard Chris's story from Jenna, how Chris had been a total burnout until he'd met his girlfriend, Maura Kennedy. He'd given up plenty of bad habits to win over Maura and her Sunday-school-teaching father, and in the process he'd completely changed his attitude about life. Melanie wasn't sure now what she'd expected the tattoo to be. Some sort of animal, maybe. A random design. Even a skull and bones.

But a cross? Wasn't that pretty extreme?

Chris smiled at her. "I had that done a couple of years ago, after I got baptized. I wanted to remember, you know? I didn't want to get to some point in my life where Christianity wasn't convenient and convince myself I was never that committed in the first place—like it was all a phase or something." He shrugged. "This way I can never delude myself longer than my next shower."

"I—I see," she stammered, wishing she did. She couldn't even have said exactly why his tattoo had surprised her so much. It wasn't as if half the celebrities in America didn't wear crosses all over their bodies. But Chris was a real person, one who had lived a hard life, and his made a bigger impact.

"I'm, um . . . I'm reading the Bible now," she volunteered, catching herself off guard.

Chris chuckled. "You'd better watch out," he teased. "That's how it starts."

"I'm just reading," she said defensively.

"And I'm just kidding. But it's hard to read the Bible and come away with nothing. It changes you, even if you don't think it will."

"I'm only curious," she said, glancing at the kids. They were still painting, oblivious. "All I know about Christianity is stuff people have told me. I think I'll be better off figuring it out for myself."

"Maybe. But Christianity's bigger than the Bible. I mean, the Bible's important, but it isn't God. Sooner or later, you have to look up from those pages, and if you're lucky, maybe you see him. Just a glimpse. You know?"

"I guess," she answered dubiously.

"Don't tell Maura I said that," Chris added. "She'd probably have a heart attack."

Melanie laughed. "It's easy for people like Maura and Peter. Raised in the church all their lives . . . They just believe everything without question. They have no idea what the rest of us go through."

He shrugged one shoulder. "I used to think that too, but now I'm not so sure. In a way, I almost think they miss out on something—the chance to choose faith for themselves. It's hard, I'll give you that, but it's incredible, too, to make that decision on your own."

Melanie felt her skin erupt into goose bumps. She had never thought of it that way before. She was about to ask Chris something else when a sudden crash sounded inside.

"Dude!" a boy's voice yelled. "You are *so* not swimming!"

Melanie spun around to see the entire first table collapsed to the floor, paint spilled everywhere.

"He did it!" three voices yelled in unison, fingers pointing at each other.

Chris sprinted past her, everything else forgotten. "I want all of you out of here *now!*" he ordered, not bothering to ask what had happened. There was no getting a straight story in situations like these anyway. "Line up outside and wait for me!"

The campers filed past Melanie on their way out the door, a contrite little troop.

"Sorry," Chris said, bringing up the rear. "If you want, I'll stay and help clean up. I could go find Peter to take back these boys. . . ."

"No, I'll get it," she told him. "I don't mind."

She watched Chris and his group file across the clearing, then turned to start cleaning the cabin, the goose bumps slowly flattening on her legs.

"Did you get that last part?" Kara asked Nicole, attempting to walk through the steps their squad had supposedly just learned. "And I thought things moved too fast during tryouts!"

"That choreographer zips right along," Nicole agreed, silently thanking Melanie for all the secret coaching she'd provided during tryouts. The lessons Nicole had learned then were proving invaluable now. "I think I got it, though."

She did the steps for Kara, concentrating hard on making every move perfect.

"Is *that* how that part goes?" Becca asked. "Can I do it with you guys?" She jumped in and started practicing too, while the rest of the squad looked on.

"That's not how she showed us," Debbie Morris said abruptly, stopping Nicole cold.

Had she made some mistake? Nicole ran frantically back through the moves in her mind, trying to see where she'd gone wrong. "No . . . I think that's right," she ventured at last.

"That choreographer should have stayed until we were positive we had it," Lou Anne complained, casting an annoyed look in the direction the woman had departed. "For as much as we paid to come here, they treat us like cattle."

"Don't worry," Angela said. "When Sandra gets back with our drinks, she'll know how it goes."

Jamila shrugged. "I don't know what the fuss is about. Nicole's already got it. Do it again, Nicole."

Nicole took a deep breath and snapped off the new steps with everyone watching, praying she wouldn't mess up.

"That looked perfect to me," Tanya said. She turned to Debbie. "What's wrong with it?"

"It's just . . ." Debbie rolled her eyes and flipped one dismissive wrist. "She did it different this time."

"No, she didn't," said Jamila. "She did it exactly the same."

"Maybe you ought to pay more attention, Debbie," said Sidney.

Or just keep your big mouth shut, Nicole thought triumphantly, making sure the smile on her face was extra sweet. By the time Sandra made her way back to the playing field, lugging two plastic shopping bags full of drinks, the entire squad was practicing the new steps, following Nicole's lead.

"Looking good!" Sandra said, setting the bag on the grass. "Way to keep those arms crisp, Nicole!"

Nicole beamed as everyone crowded around their coach, dying of thirst after so much exercise. Sandra began handing out bottles of Gatorade.

"Do you want orange or blue?" she asked Nicole.

Nicole shook her head; Gatorade was full of calories. "Do you have anything diet?"

"No, I have Gatorade. And you'd better drink one, because it's hot out here."

"Hurry up," Kara said. "I'm thirsty."

Nicole grabbed a blue one and scuttled out of the way. There was no point in causing a scene over something as lame as a sports drink, especially not when she was making such good progress at winning the squad over.

Besides, it is awfully hot.

Twisting the cap off the bottle, Nicole took a sip of the unnaturally colored drink. It tasted better than she had expected, sweet and icy cold. The swallows started going down faster, so smoothly that by the time she paused again, half the bottle was gone.

Nicole hesitated, looked at the calorie count on the label, then started gulping again.

I'll work it off this afternoon, she thought. *I wonder if they're having frozen yogurt at lunchtime again?*

Nine

"What were you talking to David about?" Jenna asked on Thursday as Melanie walked off the landward end of the dock, passing her on the shore.

Melanie paused, a surprised look in her green eyes. "Just getting my lifeguarding assignment."

Jenna nodded, but she'd noticed that Melanie was always the last one on the dock when David handed out those assignments—and that there was an awful lot of laughing and hair tossing going on.

"He's cute, isn't he?" Jenna asked abruptly.

Melanie's brows shot up. "I can see why you think so. Looking at David's like seeing Peter through some sort of time machine. But aren't you already taken?" Melanie glanced back at the dock, where Caitlin was just starting to walk out onto the boards, supporting Sarah by one elbow. "More importantly, isn't he?"

"I didn't . . . I mean, I wasn't . . . ," Jenna said, blushing. "Yes. We're *both* already taken."

Melanie smiled and sauntered off to the position

she'd been assigned down the shore. Jenna's eyes followed her all the way there—past Peter, who nodded, past Leah, who waved, and past Jesse, who gave her a truly sullen look.

She probably wasn't really flirting, Jenna reassured herself as Melanie took her position. David blew the signal, and all the kids charged from the shore down into the water. *I mean, who* wouldn't *like David? She was just being friendly*.

Still, for her sister's sake, Jenna wouldn't mind if Melanie acted a little colder. *Although, if David were interested, would he have sent her all the way down the beach?* Jenna smiled and relaxed. *I'm probably still a little oversensitive where Melanie's concerned*.

Putting Melanie out of her mind, Jenna did an automatic scan for swimmers in trouble before letting her eyes drift back to the dock. Caitlin was sitting halfway to the end with her bare legs dangling in the water, watching Sarah zigzag back and forth on a blue kickboard. David stood at the very end, a red rescue tube at the ready and a silver whistle around his neck. With so many campers in the water, he needed to keep his attention on the kids instead of his girlfriend. Even so, Jenna could feel the pull between them. Their eyes were on other tasks, but she knew their minds were on each other.

As she watched, David turned his head Caitlin's way and winked. Caitlin smiled in greeting, then looked shyly at her knees. A moment later, she glanced at him again from the corners of her eyes. He grinned back happily.

Those two are so gone, Jenna thought happily, forcing her gaze back to her duties. Some of the boys were dunking each other, but there was nothing new about that. No point in getting wet unless someone stopped coming back up. A group of girls was splashing a bit farther out, playing some ongoing game of pretend involving freshwater mermaids.

Caitlin and David—who'd have believed it? Not only that, but the way things were going, the shyest of the Conrad sisters stood a good chance of being the first one engaged.

I really hope they get married, Jenna thought, imagining how exciting a wedding would be. She and her sisters would all be bridesmaids, of course, and now that she and Caitlin were closer than Caitlin and Mary Beth, Jenna might even get to be maid of honor! In her mind, she pictured the perfect wedding, superimposing it over the real-life havoc in the water. Caitlin would wear white, of course; David, black. The bridesmaids' dresses would be peach. No, mint green. No, pink.

Or what about aqua? Jenna's eyebrows rose with interest. She had never been to a wedding with aqua bridesmaids' dresses.

Because there aren't any aqua flowers, she realized a moment later. *Still . . . the flowers could be all white. Or peach, or pink, or something that blended in.*

The scene in her mind became more elaborate as she added detail after detail: summer hats for the bridesmaids, a tiara to hold Caitlin's veil, little bags filled with birdseed to throw at the happy couple as they ran out of church.

And the tables at the reception should be draped in aqua too. With centerpieces to match the bridesmaids' bouquets and—

"You stop it, Danny Butler, or I'll clobber you!" Priscilla's angry voice rang out.

Jenna sighed. That little tomboy could do it, too.

Spotting the altercation, Jenna waded in up to her thighs, anxious to smooth things over before they got worse. "What's the problem?" she asked.

"He dunked me!" Priscilla accused, pointing at Danny.

"I did not!" Danny hollered back. "She was in the way."

"It's not our fault if she gets in the way," Jason shouted, gleefully joining the argument.

"We're playing a game," Priscilla said, her brown eyes narrowing to slits. "We need to swim through here."

"Oooh, I'm a mermaid!" Danny mocked her, throwing himself around the water like a wounded porpoise. "Oooh, I'm so pretty! I guess you'd *have* to pretend that part," he added, sending Jason into fits of rude laughter.

Priscilla brandished two clenched fists.

"Do you all want to go sit under the flagpole?" Jenna asked quickly. "Because that's where you'll end up if you can't stop fighting."

"Tell them to leave us alone!" Priscilla demanded, her circle of friends clustering behind her.

"Tell *them* to stay out of our way!" Danny insisted, pointing.

Jenna was relieved to see Peter walking into the water to join them.

"Listen up!" he said, raising one hand to ward off further lies and explanations. "Danny, you and your friends stay here between Jenna and the dock. Priscilla, you girls go play your game out in front of Jesse."

The boys jeered because the girls were the ones being relocated. Priscilla put her hands to her hips, her features twisting at the unfairness of it all.

"Us! Why do *we* have to move?" she whined.

"Because I want these clowns closer to the head lifeguard," Peter said, nodding toward the boys. "If anyone's going to need rescuing, it's them."

The girls left happily after that, trailing triumphant giggles in their wakes. It was the boys' turn to grumble as they resumed their dunking war with something less than their former enthusiasm.

"Way to go, Supercounselor!" Jenna told Peter, smiling. "I'm never sure how to handle things when the kids get like that."

"When they *get* like that?" Peter rolled his eyes.

"They're *always* like that lately. They were never this much trouble at the park."

"Maybe because you only had them four hours a week," she suggested.

Peter sighed. "Maybe."

"Besides, camp's getting easier," she said, sensing he could use some building up. "Things are starting to fall into place. And the kids love coming here."

"Do you think so?" he asked earnestly. "Because sometimes I really wonder."

"Of course! How could you doubt it?"

He sighed again. "I'm exhausted."

"You've been working too hard, that's all. I tell you what—tonight, after dinner, come to my house and I'll make a peach pie. The tree out back is loaded, and the fruit's so sweet you won't believe it. We can watch TV while the pie's in the oven." She smiled. "If we're lucky, we might even get the den to ourselves."

"Sounds like heaven. I'll bring the ice cream."

He walked up to his post on the shore and Jenna returned to hers, thoughts of peaches and Peter mixing with the wedding scene still lingering in her head until eventually she became the bride, cutting a cake with perfect peach-colored frosting flowers. Peter stood at her side, all grown up and achingly handsome in his black tux, smiling as he fed her the first piece.

It could happen, she thought dreamily, returning his imagined smile. *Someday . . .*

"Whatcha doing there, buddy? Did you find a frog?" Ben asked, floating into the shallows behind his favorite camper. The reedy water where Elton was standing barely lapped at the hem of his bathing suit. Ben pulled himself along the muddy bottom with his hands to avoid having to stand and adjust to the air temperature.

"I can't find any," Elton returned, disappointed. His skin was still the color of milk despite nearly two weeks in the sun, and his little-boy's belly jutted over the waistband of his red shorts.

"Maybe I can help you look." Ben pulled in a little closer.

"Don't you have to be a lifeguard today, Counselor Ben?"

"Nah. I thought I did, but they already have enough people onshore."

Ben had volunteered to stand watch with Peter anyway, just for the added safety, but Peter had insisted that Ben go swimming. "Play with the kids," he'd said. "Or just paddle around and relax. We're only getting in each other's way up here."

"I don't think there *are* any frogs in this stupid lake," Elton said sulkily, crossing his arms on the shelf of his belly.

"There must be." But Ben's mind wasn't truly on amphibians. All he could think about was how different Elton and Bernie looked. "If your sister was here, I'll bet she could help us find one."

Elton looked at him as if he were nuts. Maybe frogs weren't Bernie's favorite. Ben filed the fact away for potential future use.

"Is she going to be at the library again this weekend?" Ben asked.

Milk-white shoulders twitched. "I dunno. Counselor Ben, why can't I look over there?" Elton pointed to the farthest end of the cove, where a tangle of logs had been ruled off-limits. "If I were a frog, that's where I'd be."

"You know Peter doesn't want you kids playing in those logs. Too dangerous."

"But if you come with me . . . ," Elton wheedled.

That ought to be all right, Ben thought, weighing the possibility. Nothing bad could happen to Elton while Ben was there to watch him. It was on the tip of his tongue to say yes when another thought occurred to him.

But what if something did happen to Elton? And I was in charge when it did? Bernie would never speak to me again!

Not that he had any strong evidence she was going to anyway. Lunch the weekend before had been a blast. They'd really seemed to hit it off, and their shared interest in computers had given them something to talk about. But Bernie had left for home immediately after they'd finished eating, and Ben hadn't seen or heard from her since.

Which doesn't necessarily mean all is lost. She isn't likely to contact me unless I make the first move. But what move? How?

"What?" Ben said, suddenly aware that Elton was staring at him with both hands on his hips.

"The logs?" Elton reminded him. "Why can't we?"

Ben shook his head. "Sorry, bud. A rule's a rule. But I'll give you a ride on my back if you want."

He offered his wet back, and after a moment Elton climbed on, wrapping both arms in a crushing grip around Ben's windpipe.

"Okay," Ben said, gasping as he tried to insert his hands between Elton's arms and his throat. "A little air, please, if you don't want your sea horse to suffocate."

Elton giggled.

"You won't think it's so funny when I drop dead and you're out in the middle of the lake by yourself."

The arms loosened immediately. Elton wasn't much of a swimmer.

Ben pushed along the bottom with his toes until he reached chest-deep water and then began bounding along parallel to the shoreline.

"Does your sister have a boyfriend?" he blurted out.

"No!" Elton snorted. Ben couldn't see Elton's face, but his little friend sounded appalled. "Ick! Who would want her?"

I would, Ben answered silently. But Bernie would probably never be interested in him that way.

Would she?

Maybe . . . if I can keep her thinking I'm some sort of cool older guy with lots of experience. Ben pursed his lips. *Which is to say, if I can keep her from finding out who I really am . . .*

"Faster!" Elton demanded, letting go with one arm to slap Ben's sunburned shoulder. The unexpected pain jolted Ben back to Earth with a yelp.

"Come on, horsie! You're slow!"

"Look at that dress!" Nicole said, taking the cherry Blow-Pop out of her mouth and pointing it at the magazine Kara was reading.

They were both belly-down on the carpet, along with Becca, Sidney, Jamila, and Angela, the six of them splayed out like spokes on a wheel, the center of which held all the extra suckers and jawbreakers Nicole had brought and a stack of her cheerleading magazines. Behind them, Tanya and Lou Anne had claimed the lower bunk bed, while latecomers Debbie and Maria had to settle for chairs. It was the squad's last night at Camp Twist-n-Shout, so the girls were staying up late, hanging out in their pajamas and making every minute count.

Jamila's gaze followed Nicole's sucker. "Is that a dress or a Band-Aid?" she asked scornfully.

"Exactly!" Nicole gloated. "It's not even an *attractive* Band-Aid!"

A few of the girls chuckled. Becca reached for another sucker. They'd been pigging out all night, eating through the rest of the candy Nicole had brought from home, reading Nicole's magazines, and choosing Nicole's room as their primary hangout. Maybe their presence was supposed to be some sort of present for her seventeenth birthday. Nicole didn't know—all she knew was that she was in heaven.

"There's chocolate in that blue bag under the bed," she told Tanya, turning her head toward the bunks. "Pull it out if you want some."

Tanya groaned. "I couldn't."

"I could. Toss it here," Maria instructed.

Tanya dug out a bag of Hershey's Kisses and threw it over the circle to Maria, who was wearing a long pink nightshirt with calico numbers on it. Maria's boyfriend was a Wildcat, and she had sewn his number on her nightshirt front and back, just like a football jersey.

Cute, Nicole thought again, still not quite over her pajama envy. Not that her own weren't cute too.

They're adorable, she corrected herself, admiring them surreptitiously. They had cost way too much for flannel shorties—her mom had made sure she knew that—but Nicole had fallen in love with the campy print of fried eggs, telephones, and steaming cups of coffee the moment she had seen them. They were absolutely cool, even if they didn't have some gorgeous football player's jersey numbers on them. Not that Noel Phillips was a conquest to be taken lightly, but still . . .

Maybe next time, she thought. There were sure to be more slumber parties—and conquests—before the coming school year was over.

"What time is it?" Tanya asked abruptly.

Nicole glanced at her watch. "Ten-thirty. You're not going to bed now! We're just getting started!"

"No, I . . . I have to go to the bathroom. Come with me, Angela."

The two of them left, and Maria immediately plopped into the warm spot Angela had vacated on the floor.

"Finally!" she said happily, reaching for a magazine. "I couldn't see anything up there."

"No? Do you want to see too, Debbie?" Nicole asked sweetly. "We might be able to squeeze in one more."

"Never mind," Debbie said disdainfully, walking over to join Lou Anne on the bed.

Nicole smiled smugly and returned her attention to Kara's magazine.

"What do you think of this dress?" Kara asked, having turned to another page.

"I like it!" Nicole declared. The fact that she couldn't picture mousy Kara wearing it was something she chose not to mention. Kara had been nice to her when the rest of the squad had been nasty; no matter how popular Nicole got, she intended to remember that.

"Let me see," Sidney demanded.

Maria and Jamila were critiquing the model's makeup when Nicole's dorm room door burst open.

"Surprise!" Tanya, Angela, and Sandra yelled in unison.

The coach stood in the open doorway, flanked by Tanya and Angela, a cake with glowing candles cradled in her arms. Tanya led the singing: "*Happy birthday to you . . .*"

Nicole scrambled to her feet along with everyone else as the squad finished the song in perfect unison. "Oh, you guys. You didn't have to. This is the best!" she cried, her eyes filling with happy tears.

Angela produced a carton of ice cream from behind her back. "And it just keeps getting better. Rocky road. Yum!"

Tanya set up plates and plastic silverware while Sandra cleared enough makeup off Nicole's desk to put down the birthday cake.

"We all pitched in to buy the cake, and Sandra went and got it in the van," Kara explained, obviously pleased by how well the surprise had gone off. "Blow out your candles," she added.

Nicole shuffled over, hands still shaking with the thrill, drew a deep breath, then froze. There were eighteen candles on the cake.

"Uh, you guys? Thanks for the compliment, but I'm only seventeen. We need to take one off."

She reached to remove the nearest candle, but Sandra grabbed her by the wrist. "There *are* seventeen—plus one for luck. What kind of wolves were you raised with?"

"I—I never heard of that," Nicole admitted, blowing out the candles while the rest of the squad debated the proper number.

Tanya began cutting massive chunks of cake and lifting them onto plates beside Angela's scoops of ice cream. "Eat up, everyone," she said. "Whatever we can't finish has to go in the trash. Here you go, Nicole."

Nicole took the plate Tanya handed her, then stood eyeing its contents uneasily. The cake was chocolate with buttercream frosting an inch thick in the clusters of green-and-gold roses. A mountain of rocky road ice cream sat melting beside the cake, soaking into the crumbs.

How many calories on this plate? Nicole wondered. *Eight hundred? A thousand?*

She had already eaten more candy that day than in the entire month before camp. Not to mention the hamburgers and frozen yogurt and sugary drinks that kept turning up everywhere. The last thing she needed was a platter of ice cream and cake.

"Eat up!" Tanya repeated. "You only turn seventeen once."

"That's true," Nicole said slowly, picking up her fork. Everyone else was already digging in . . . and could a little birthday cake really do that much additional damage?

Besides, it would be rude not to eat it, she realized. *It would be incredibly rude, in fact.*

That settled, she dropped cross-legged to the floor beside Kara and started shoveling it in, bite after delicious bite. She vaguely remembered eating this way before, back in the dark, chubby days before her diet, but that had been a long time ago.

My diet's already out the window this week anyway, she thought, trying not to obsess about the fact that she hadn't been able to weigh herself all week. Maybe she really *was* working off all the extra calories, but she still couldn't shake the feeling that her hip bones just weren't as sharp as they had been on Monday.

Oh, well, she thought, taking another huge bite. *I'll find out what the damage is when I get home tomorrow, and until then I'm just not going to worry about it. I have all summer to slim back down!*

Ten

"I don't know why you always put me so far down the shore," Melanie complained to David Altmann. Everyone else had already received their lifeguard assignments and left, but, as usual, she was the last to get hers. "Most of the kids swim over here, closer to the dock."

David shrugged his tan shoulders. He was only slightly taller than Peter, but their age difference really showed in the amount of muscle David carried. "I must trust you, then," he said, "to give you a station it will take me so long to get to."

Melanie couldn't suppress a pleased smile. Maybe he was just flattering her, but it was still a good answer.

"Sure, *that's* the reason," she teased, tossing her hair. "You put me in Siberia because I'm the best."

"If it really bothers you, next week I'll swap you and Jenna."

"Okay," she said eagerly. There was a lot more action next to the dock, and she was getting truly bored, always guarding on the fringes.

"I just thought maybe you'd rather be next to Jesse," David added.

Melanie's jaw worked silently. "Wh—wh—what made you think that?" she finally got out. She and Jesse were becoming more intense by the day—but not at camp. Never in front of other people.

"It just seems obvious."

"Obvious?" she croaked.

"Well, sure. I mean, Jenna's with Peter, and Leah's with Miguel . . . so who does that leave for you? Call me crazy, but I can't quite see you with Ben."

"Ben!" she exhaled, throwing back her head to laugh with relief. "No. Not going to happen."

"I didn't think so. Anyway, you'd better get moving, because I'm letting these kids in the water now."

David lifted his whistle and blew the long blast that signaled the beginning of swimming. The campers lined up on the shore screamed with excitement and began rushing into the water despite the gathering clouds overhead. Thundershowers were a definite possibility, but meanwhile the heat and humidity continued to build, making a swim in the cool lake doubly attractive.

"See you later," Melanie told David, dragging her feet reluctantly down the dock. She would much rather have stayed in the middle of the fun; even though her station was supposedly next to Jesse's, they were still too far apart to do her any good.

Oh, well. Maybe Amy will come hang out with me

again. Her little friend was becoming increasingly involved with the girls her own age, though, leaving less time for Melanie. Melanie reminded herself that that was a good thing. *For Amy*.

Even though most of the kids were now in the water, none were swimming in Melanie's area. She increased her pace along the shoreline anyway, wanting to be there if finally actually needed. Still, she couldn't resist slowing down as she passed Jesse, just to say hello.

"Hey, handsome," she greeted him, keeping her voice low. "What's a hot guy like you doing standing around all by himself?"

"Watching my girlfriend flirt with Captain Baywatch over there, that's what," he returned irritably.

"What?"

"You're over there every day, I swear."

"So is everyone else! I was just getting my assignment."

"Which never changes, so why bother? What was he saying to you?"

"Nothing!"

Jesse's eyes narrowed suspiciously.

"I mean, just stuff. Nothing important."

Jesse would be sure to make a big deal out of David's pairing them up, as if everyone else must be thinking the same thing. He wouldn't understand the comment as the meaningless shot in the dark that it was.

"You sure seemed to think it was funny," he said bitterly. "Is that why you don't want to tell people about us? Because it might hurt your chances with *him?*"

"*What?*" Melanie could hardly believe her ears. "I don't even *have* a chance with him!"

"But you want one."

"No!"

"You were flirting!"

"I was not! Can't I even talk to another guy?"

"Maybe it's the way you do it," Jesse said, tilting back his head and shaking out an imaginary mane of hair. "Oh, David, you're *so* funny!" he said in a high falsetto.

"That's it," she snapped, glancing down the beach to see if anyone had noticed. "I am not having this conversation."

"I don't want you talking to him."

"You what?" She raised her eyebrows, amazed. "Sorry, but you don't get to tell me what to do. I'll talk to whoever I want."

"*Flirt* with whoever you want, you mean."

That he could even accuse her of being into someone else . . . that he would try to *control* her . . .

"If that's what you think, then maybe we should just forget about being together," she said furiously.

"Maybe we should," he shot back.

"Fine!" she exclaimed, stalking off down the beach. *I knew it!* she thought. *I knew something like this would happen sooner or later.* She and Jesse did great when no one else was around, but they couldn't live in a vacuum forever.

I was so right not to let him run around telling everyone about us. Jesse hasn't changed a bit!

I survived the first two weeks, Peter congratulated himself, checking his watch. There were only twenty minutes of swimming left; then the kids would take turns getting dressed in the cabin, they'd have a quick closing assembly, and everyone would pile into the bus for the ride back to town. *I can make it that long.*

And that was when he saw the first bolt of lightning crack the sky on the far side of the lake, closely followed by a boom of thunder. David's whistle blasted next, sounding the emergency signal for everyone to get out of the water. The kids began surging onto the shore just as the clouds opened up above them and the rain came pouring down.

"Everyone, go to the cabin!" Peter shouted, cupping his hands to be heard over the chaos. The kids were running around in the rain, squealing as if they hadn't just come out of the water anyway, when an even closer explosion of thunder ended in an ominous rumble of echoes. "Now!"

He could hear David shouting the same thing from the dock, threatening the stragglers with dire consequences if they didn't move fast. Melanie and the other counselors were all running in from their posts toward the center of the cove, sweeping the kids along with them.

"Get to the cabin! Now!" Peter repeated, pointing.

Jenna ran up to him, her long hair dripping and her cheeks still pink from the heat that was only now breaking. "Aren't you coming?"

"As soon as I'm sure we've got everyone. Start a head count at the cabin."

She nodded and ran off, nearly losing her balance in the mud that was already forming. The bare dirt of the clearing was so dry that the sudden downpour didn't have time to soak in but mixed with the surface dust in a layer that both slipped underfoot and stuck to whatever it touched. The ground was punctuated with dry holes left by the feet that had run over it, the occasional long swaths from people's slips providing the exclamation points.

I hope someone makes those kids wipe their feet, Peter thought, running over to meet David as his brother abandoned the dock.

"Is everyone accounted for?" David asked, holding a rescue tube over his head to deflect the pouring rain. The heavy droplets bounced off the red vinyl surface and spattered his face anyway.

"I think so. Jenna's doing a head count at the cabin to be sure."

Another bolt sliced the sky, arcing toward the center of the lake. The thunder was simultaneous.

"Let's get up there too," David shouted. "It's dangerous standing here."

The brothers tore across the clearing, throwing up divots of mud and arriving just behind the final campers.

"Wipe your feet!" Peter yelled, but no one was listening. Kids packed into the little building as fast as they could, some beginning to cry as the storm became more frightening. "At least knock off the big hunks!"

But when Peter got inside, he saw it was no use. The cabin floor was an inch deep in dirt, the water running off more than forty people quickly turning the soil into slurry. Steam rose from wet bodies and condensed on the windowpanes, obscuring the view outside. The whole scene was so surreal he could barely believe it was happening.

Leah shouted to be heard over the din. "All right, you guys! Nobody's hurt, so please stop shouting and simmer down."

In the corner, Jenna had climbed onto a folding chair and was counting heads from above. She flashed him a thumbs-up when she finished, and Peter breathed a sigh of relief. The kids might be dirty, but at least they were safe.

"All right! Stop yelling!" Leah yelled again.

Jesse leaned against a wall, scowling and doing nothing, as if barely aware of the panic around him.

Miguel waded through the crowd to get to Peter,

the weather radio clutched to his ear. "They're saying this could last a couple more hours," he reported.

"Great," Peter said with a groan. "How are we all going to stay in here two hours?"

The crafts tables and chairs had been stacked against the wall before swimming, standard procedure now so that the kids could have more room to change, but space was still so tight that the counselors never sent more than two groups into the cabin at a time. Now all five were elbow to elbow, along with seven counselors and a lifeguard. There was no room to dress, no room to sit down. There was barely room to breathe.

"Open the windows," Peter directed, feeling suddenly claustrophobic. "Let's get some air in here."

"The rain will come in!" Ben protested.

Melanie made a face. "Like it matters."

The windows were opened, and the noise in the cabin gradually died down as the kids became more interested in watching the storm light the sky outside. Miguel and Jenna worked the room, reassuring the ones who were still scared.

David looked at Peter and shook his head. "Now what?"

"Good question," Peter admitted.

They couldn't leave the kids standing around in wet bathing suits indefinitely, but there was no way for them to change in such tight quarters—not to mention the unfortunate coed angle. On top of that, the campers' clothes were in their backpacks, which were all in the lean-to cupboard around back. If they could only get their stuff and get to the bus, they could change in the buildings at Clearwater Crossing Park—but first they had to get there. Peter peeked outside again. Was the rain getting lighter, or was that wishful thinking?

"The first good break in the clouds, we run for it," he announced. "If it looks clear and there isn't any lightning, we go. They can change back at the park."

David nodded. There wasn't much else they could do.

Peter stood on a chair and explained the plan to the kids, who seemed excited by the unexpected change in routine. Instead of complaining, they started boasting about who'd get to the bus first.

"It's not a race!" Peter added, but the boys were already betting each other and the girls, and Peter had to admit that he didn't really care. Anything to keep them occupied until a break in the storm came.

Half an hour later, he finally saw his chance.

"All right! Listen up!" he called from the vantage point of the chair, breaking into Counselor Ben's forty-fifth attempt at "Row, Row, Row Your Boat" in rounds. "Each group follow your counselor around to get your backpacks from David, put on your shoes, and walk directly to the bus. No lollygagging and no racing, either. Just get your stuff and get on the bus. Got it?"

By then the kids were bored and uncomfortable and as eager to get home as he was. They did a reasonable job of filing out in order while Peter kept his eye on the sky and prayed the rain would wait until everyone was safely on the bus. He led his own group out last and locked the cabin door. They could shovel the place out on Monday.

Or I suppose I could come back and clean it this weekend . . . but I'm not gonna, he decided, helping his boys pull shoes onto wet feet. *I need a break in a big way.*

At last they were on the trail, picking their way up and down the now slippery slopes while the break in the clouds held. Through gaps in the trees, Peter could sometimes glimpse Jenna's group dead ahead and Leah's in front of hers. All of a sudden, a girl's scream rang out, followed by a loud, anguished wail. Peter's heart lurched into his throat. He instinctively began running, his campers following hard on his heels.

"No, stay back," he yelled. "It's slippery. You're all going to fall down." They didn't listen, of course, and he didn't stop to make them, too worried that he already had some sort of injury on his hands.

"What happened? What happened?" he shouted as he tore through Jenna's group. Topping a rise, he came upon Leah's.

"It's nothing!" Leah reassured him. "Lisa slipped and fell in a puddle, that's all."

Peter backpedaled at the top of the hill, narrowly avoiding the same fate. The section of trail they were on went into the saddle between two low hills, and the soil was scarred with the muddy furrows made by sliding sneakers. At the bottom of the dip, where the storm water had collected, Lisa sat in a puddle of what looked like loose chocolate pudding. Mud dripped from her bare arms and plastered ringlets, the tracks of her furious tears making her face an even bigger mess.

"Aw, *cool!*" Peter heard Jason exclaim behind him.

Then, before Peter could stop him, almost before he realized what was about to happen, Jason took three running steps from the hilltop and flung himself onto his belly.

"Wheeee!" he screamed, rocketing face first down the path as if it were covered in snow. He splashed into Lisa's puddle, sending a second wave of mud right at her.

"I hate you, Jason Fairchild!" she screamed, throwing twin handfuls of ooze at him. It was a wasted effort—the only clean things on Jason were the whites of his thrilled eyes.

Within a second the other boys had followed Jason's lead, sliding and splashing into the puddle, whooping it up the whole way.

"Stop it! Stop it right now!" Peter finally found his voice to shout, but it was wasted effort. The more adventurous of Jenna's girls joined in, while Leah's scrambled to get back up the hill and try their own luck. Jesse's and Miguel's groups came running back from the other direction, curious about the commotion, and they started sliding too.

"I give up," Peter groaned, squeezing his aching temples.

Leah chuckled beside him. "Does the word 'Woodstock' mean anything to you?"

"Yes. Ha, ha. Very funny." He'd seen the famous pictures. "What am I supposed to do now?"

She shrugged. "What can you do? We'll just have to round them up and put them on the bus."

"Like that?" he groaned, imagining the mess.

There were no showers, though, and he couldn't risk putting the kids back in the lake with the sky still threatening lightning. In the end, he did exactly as Leah had suggested, wincing as every muddy camper climbed the stairs, cringing as nearly forty filthy rear ends plopped onto the vinyl seats. To help him out, Melanie had joined the counselors riding back in the bus instead of driving home with Jesse, but no amount of extra counseling could avert the inevitable. By the time Peter herded the kids off the bus at the other end of the line, the floor was caked with drying mud, every seat was filthy, and the interior walls, windows, and even the ceiling were smeared with long brown streaks.

So much for taking a break this weekend, Peter thought, surveying the damage while David led the kids through the park in search of a hose. *I'll probably be cleaning this bus all day tomorrow.*

Exhausted, discouraged, and more than a little sorry for himself, he sank down on the top bus stair, not even caring that now his shorts were dirty too.

What in the world made me think that running a camp would be fun?

"C-C-H-S! Goooooooooooooo, Wildcats!"

The noise in the van was deafening as Sandra drove into Clearwater Crossing Friday night, all ten cheerleaders shouting at once.

"All right! Enough!" Sandra called at the break between cheers. "I'm glad you're so fired up, but I'd like to be able to hear tomorrow."

Nicole laughed gleefully, feeling on top of the world. She was a cheerleader, she was seventeen, and she was totally, completely part of the squad.

"Does anyone want more licorice?" she asked, passing around her last box of Red Vines. She helped herself to one more stick before she did, thinking it might soothe her throat after so much shouting.

"I see the high school," Angela announced from the front seat. Earlier that day, Tanya had made her the squad's official second-in-command, awarding her shotgun privileges for the ride home. "The parking lot lights are on."

Good, thought Nicole. Since she was going to have to call her mother to come get her, at least she wouldn't be waiting around in the dark.

Seconds later, Sandra pulled the van into the center of the wide-open lot. A couple of cars were already waiting, parked haphazardly across the painted lines. Nicole envied the girls who'd be going home in those, ferried off like queens while the peasants waited for their parents.

I'm not going to let it get me down, she decided, shrugging off the inconvenience. After all, she wouldn't be waiting alone. Sandra stopped the van and everyone piled out—stiff, tired, and slightly disoriented from the long trip home. Nicole was walking to the back of the van to help unload the bags when she heard another car pull up, followed by the sound of a slamming door.

"Nicole?" a male voice called, freezing her in her tracks. It was Noel.

"Ooh, *Nicole!*" a couple of cheerleaders teased. "Your honey's here to meet you."

And he was, striding toward her, a red rose extended in his hand. "Welcome back," he said, with a smile that melted her to her toes. "Happy birthday, too."

"Thanks." Somehow she managed not to sound completely amazed. "I, uh, didn't expect to see you here."

He shrugged charmingly. "That's why it's a surprise. Are you ready to go home?"

He's here to drive *me*, she realized. *I'm not a peasant. I'm one of the queens!*

And she felt royal in every cell of her body as Noel loaded her bags into his black sports car under the envious gaze of her teammates.

"Okay?" he asked. "Did you say good-bye to everybody?"

"Good-bye!" Nicole called grandly, waving from beside his car.

"See you, Nicole!" Becca called back with a jealous look.

Noel opened her car door and Nicole climbed in. She expected him to shut it quickly, but instead he leaned over its top, grinning down at her.

"So," he drawled, his face only inches from hers. "Do you have to go straight home?"

Eleven

"Thanks for helping me do this," Peter said again as Ben and Jesse climbed back into the bus carrying fresh buckets of water. "Can you believe this mess?"

"It looks like a strip club held its mud-wrestling contest in here," Jesse said, but he didn't smile. He had agreed to help out the moment Peter had asked him, but he'd been sulking ever since he got there.

"We should have made the kids who started the mud sliding clean the bus," Ben said, resuming his washing of the ceiling while Jesse returned to the windows. "It would have taught them a good lesson."

Peter sighed and rested on the push broom he was using to half sweep, half scrape the rock-hard clods of dried mud off the floor. "It would have taught *someone* a lesson, anyway. Can you really imagine spending the day making Jason and Danny do this job right? I'd rather do it myself."

"Maybe this is kind of easier," Ben admitted.

For a while there was no sound in the bus except for Peter's broom and the dripping of water as Ben and Jesse dunked their sponges over and over. Peter's mind wandered, thinking of all the things he would rather be doing. He could be hanging out with Jenna or playing tennis with David. He could be enjoying his mother's cooking for lunch instead of looking forward to the baloney sandwich steaming up its Baggie on the dashboard. The bus was parked in some shade at the edge of the lot, but the day was so oppressively humid that the heat seemed to come from every direction, not just overhead.

"I could help you some more after we finish this," Ben volunteered, breaking the silence at last. "I mean, like, if you have some papers you need driven around to all the campers' houses, I can take them for you."

"What kind of papers?" Peter asked, baffled.

"Well, you know . . . like if you need some permission slips signed or something."

Peter shook his head. "All the permission slips were signed before camp started. There's nothing I need signed now."

"Oh." Ben stood on a seat to wipe a particularly nasty-looking smear off the bus's curved metal ceiling. "There's all that lost-and-found stuff, though."

"What about it?" Peter asked.

"*Somebody* has to return it. If you want, I can drive the basket around to everyone's houses and have their parents take a look."

"Are you serious?" To do what Ben was proposing would take easily the rest of the day, all for a few misplaced towels, a belt, and a couple of sweatshirts. "Why would you want to do that?"

"Those things cost money. I'll bet people will be glad to get them back."

Jesse had stopped working and now broke into the conversation. "It will cost you more than that stuff is worth in gas alone. Why not just keep the basket here and let people look through it when they figure out they have something missing?"

Peter was wondering the same thing. That was the system that had been in place ever since he'd started the Junior Explorers, and no one had ever complained.

"Well, you know. Service. Give the people what they want." Ben's cheeks were turning red. "It was just an idea."

"Why do you want to go to all the campers' houses?" Jesse asked suspiciously.

A deepening of Ben's blush told Peter that Jesse had hit the mark.

"I don't!" Ben protested. "I just wanted to help!" His denial was completely transparent.

"Did something go wrong with one of the kids?" Peter asked nervously. "Is there something I should know about?"

"No! Nothing like that. Forget I mentioned it."

Ben grabbed the sponge from his bucket and lifted it back to the ceiling in such a hurry that he forgot to wring it out. He barely dodged the resulting faceful of water.

"You know what I think?" Jesse asked slowly. "I think Ben has a crush on someone."

"On a *camper*? Please tell me you're kidding," Peter begged.

"No! Eew!" Ben responded immediately.

"There's someone at one of those houses," Jesse insisted. "I know the signs. Maybe someone with an older sister?"

"Elton!" Peter said immediately, remembering that he had sent Ben to the boy's house. "Elton has a sister."

"You guys," Ben whined. "What is this? The Clearwater Inquisition?"

"I knew it," Jesse said, satisfied. "Poor sap."

"What's that supposed to mean?" Ben asked.

Jesse shrugged, a sour look on his face. "Just that love ain't all it's cracked up to be. In fact, if you want my opinion, girls are a pain in the butt."

"Love!" Ben exclaimed wistfully. "I'd settle for *like* and a movie."

"Don't say I didn't warn you," Jesse replied cynically, starting on another window.

Peter couldn't tell if something was actually bothering him or if he was just being Jesse. He sure seemed more sullen than usual.

"What's her name again? Bernie?" Peter asked Ben. "If you like her, why not just ask her out?"

"I want to, but . . ." Ben wrung his sponge out over his shoes and didn't even seem to notice. "What if she says no?"

"What if she says yes?" Peter countered.

This is getting ridiculous, Melanie thought, checking her watch again. It was after five on Saturday evening and she still hadn't heard from Jesse. They hadn't spoken once since their absurd argument the day before.

Like I'm really going to chase David Altmann, she thought irritably, pacing back and forth in her bedroom. *Like I'd be interested! And besides, he's totally in love with Caitlin.*

So Jenna said, anyway, and that was good enough for Melanie. There were plenty of other guys in the world. Up until yesterday, she had even thought she had one.

I do! I mean, he's as much mine now as he was before. That was just a silly fight.

But then how come he hadn't called? Could he have believed she was serious when she said they should call things off?

Or maybe he just thinks I ought to be the one to apologize, Melanie thought, stopping to stare blindly out her window. *That was a pretty rude thing to say.*

On the other hand, he had agreed with her. Could *he* have been serious?

"I'm just going to call him. This is nuts."

Walking to her nightstand, she hit his speed-dial button on her phone before she could chicken out. When she heard his voice on the line, though, she wished she had taken more time to figure out what to say.

"Jesse?" she ventured. "Hi. It's me."

"Hi."

She couldn't tell if he was still mad or not.

"I just, uh, thought I'd see what you were doing. I mean, I thought you'd probably stop by or something today."

"I was helping Peter clean the bus."

"All day?"

"You saw how dirty it was. You could hardly wait to go home in it yesterday instead of riding with me."

Okay, he was still mad. She had kind of deduced that anyway.

"So what are you doing now?" she asked.

"We're about to eat dinner."

She nodded, forgetting he couldn't see her. Normal families did do things like eat meals together; it wasn't *necessarily* an excuse to get off the phone. . . .

"All right. I'll let you go, then. I just wanted to say hi." Her finger moved toward the disconnect button.

"Wait," he said before she could press it.

"What?"

"What are you doing now?"

"Nothing."

"Oh." There was a long, significant pause. "I could maybe come over later."

"Yeah, maybe." But now something new was bothering her. "Were you *ever* going to call me?"

"I don't know," he said, sounding exasperated. "Probably."

"You don't *know?*"

"Well, what do you want me to say, Melanie? You don't want to commit to being with me, you go panting after David right in front of me—"

"I was getting my lifeguard assignment!"

"Whatever. It doesn't matter."

"It does too matter! Because you don't trust me!"

"That's not what I said."

"No, but that's how you're acting."

"Or maybe that's just you, putting your interpretation on things. Maybe you have a guilty conscience."

"I do *not* have a guilty conscience because I don't have anything to—" She cut herself off and took a deep breath.

"This is why we shouldn't be together," she said, in something closer to her normal voice. "We're both too stubborn, too set in our ways. Neither one of us trusts other people."

Jesse snorted, then belatedly seemed to realized how serious she was. "So we'll change. People change, you know."

Melanie sighed. "I don't think so. This is how we are, Jesse. This is *who* we are. If you and I stayed together, it would always be this way."

"What do you mean, *if* we stayed together? What are you telling me?"

She hesitated, knowing that what she was about to say would hurt, but suddenly there were a million reasons to doubt that she and Jesse could ever have a real relationship. And Melanie wasn't interested in things that weren't real. She never had been.

"I guess I'm saying we should think about it," she told him at last. "I don't think we should see each other anymore until we're sure what we want."

"Are you kidding?" he demanded. "I already know what I want."

She sighed again. "I don't."

"What are you doing?" Caitlin asked Jenna, walking into their room Sunday afternoon. Her gray dog, Abby, trotted at her heels like a shaggy canine shadow.

Jenna hunched hurriedly over her desk, trying to cover the things spread out there. "You have to promise not to tell David."

"Why shouldn't I tell David?" Cat's light brown eyes clouded over.

"This is for Peter. For his birthday. And I don't want anything getting back to him. Promise?"

Caitlin smiled, relaxing. "I promise," she said, sitting on her bed to take off her shoes. She had just returned from making the rounds of her dog-walking business, too dedicated to quit on her elderly clients even though Jenna suspected she'd love to free up more time to spend with David.

"I'm planning a surprise birthday party for Peter at camp next Friday. He's been working hard, and he deserves something special. See?" Jenna held up one of the construction paper cards she'd just made as a model. "I'm going to have all the kids make birthday cards in crafts during the week, and then on Friday we'll have cake and ice cream. Mom said she'd drive it up in the afternoon."

Caitlin looked skeptical, a rare expression for her. "I don't know why you're worried about me telling David. One of those kids will spill the beans to Peter for sure."

"Not if I tell them I'll send back the cake and ice cream if Peter finds out about the party. That'll keep 'em quiet."

"Except that you wouldn't really do that."

"They only have to think I might," Jenna said with a smile. The last two weeks as a counselor had taught her a few tricks. "So what are you and David doing tonight? Anything special?"

Caitlin shook her head. "We're just going to walk around the trout pond at the park and see if the fish are jumping. They stocked it for the kids this week."

"Sounds romantic," Jenna said enviously. She and

Peter had both known about the pond being stocked. Why hadn't either of them thought of that?

Caitlin blushed slightly. "I think he's going to ask—"

"Hi! What are you guys doing?" Maggie interrupted, not waiting for an answer before walking into the room uninvited. Her hair was done up in two pigtails rolled into Princess Leia–style cinnamon buns over her ears—not a good look. "I'm bored," she announced. "None of my friends can come over."

"Just because the door is open doesn't mean you can waltz right in here," Jenna began. "The least you can do is—"

"Hello, Abby," Maggie said totally ignoring Jenna as she stooped to pet the dog in its bed by the closet. "Did you have a nice walk today? See anything good?"

"She's not going to answer you. She's a *dog*," Jenna grumbled, returning to the project on her desk. The best way to get rid of Maggie was to pretend she didn't exist.

But Maggie wasn't so easily thwarted. Standing up, she opened the doors of the closet Jenna and Caitlin shared and stood looking inside. "Your clothes are still too big for me, Caitlin," she said after a minute. "But I'll bet I can wear some of Jenna's now."

"I'll bet you can't!" Jenna told her, spinning her

chair back around. "You'd better stay out of my stuff."

"I'm not just going to *take* things," Maggie informed her haughtily. "I'll ask first."

"Well, pretend you just asked and I said no. Now extrapolate that for the rest of the year."

"You're so stingy!" Maggie accused, her false maturity slipping. "Why can't I borrow your stuff?"

"Because we're going to be at the same school next year, and I don't want people thinking I'm borrowing *your* stuff. Besides, you take terrible care of clothes. I used to share a room with you, remember?"

"I was only in eighth grade then!"

"You were in eighth grade two weeks ago!"

Maggie's lips pressed together angrily before she wheeled around and headed for the door. "Fine. Forget I asked. You don't have any cool clothes anyway."

"Then why you do want to wear them?" Jenna retorted to her younger sister's back.

Maggie stiffened, then ran down the stairs.

"Do you believe her?" Jenna appealed to Caitlin. "What's wrong with *her* clothes?"

Caitlin shook her head, her mind obviously on a different subject. "Was Maggie wearing makeup?"

"Was she?" Jenna returned, shocked. She hadn't looked closely enough to notice. "She'd better stay out of Mom's sight if she is."

"It's those new girls she's hanging out with. They're making themselves over every day."

"Yeah, what's that all about, anyway? She has to change her whole image just to go to high school?"

Caitlin smiled. "Apparently. It's just a stage. She'll grow out of it."

"I hope so," said Jenna, shaking her head. "Sometimes I think Maggie's been in a stage her entire life."

Twelve

"Counselor Ben? When are we going to eat?" whined Bryan. "I'm starving."

"Me too," said Elton, "and I've got a good lunch today. Meat loaf sandwich. Yum!"

Ben felt his own stomach rumble, but he did his best to ignore it. Since Miguel was at the hospital again and Nicole hadn't put herself back on the schedule yet, Peter had entrusted Ben with a group of his own that Monday. Unfortunately, he had also saddled Ben's group with a nature hike, the kids' least favorite activity. It didn't matter how gorgeous the Ozarks scenery was, or how diligently Ben pointed out the different birds and flowers; the only thing the campers had talked about from the moment they'd set out was how hot, tired, bored, and, now, hungry they were.

"Peter just makes us go on hikes when he doesn't have anything better for us to do," Lars accused.

Ben had secretly suspected the same thing, but he leapt to his friend's defense anyway. "That's not true!

He *lets* us go on hikes so that we can have fun enjoying nature."

"I've got two Ding Dongs in my lunch," Bryan said wistfully.

"Two? Lucky!" said Lars's brother, Leo. "I'll trade you my yogurt for one."

"Ding Dongs are for babies," Jamal said scornfully. "I've got homemade cherry pie."

Ben's stomach did a backflip. "Stop talking about food," he begged, checking his watch. "We're not supposed to go back for lunch for another forty minutes."

"*Forty minutes!*" The wail that went up was swift and unanimous. "We can't wait forty minutes! We're hungry *now!*"

"Why can't we go back early?" Elton asked. "We're just going to eat in our own group anyway."

"Because." Ben didn't have a better explanation.

"Geez, Counselor Ben, you never let us do anything!" said Lars.

"You're mean!" Bryan accused.

"When I was in Peter's group, we could change stuff if everybody wanted to," Blane told them. "Counselor Ben just does whatever Peter says!"

The last comment hurt, because it was true. Peter had been known to do unplanned things with his group, but Ben was afraid to deviate from the schedule the tiniest bit for fear of being bucked back to assistant status.

"Well, uh, maybe everybody *doesn't* want to go back," Ben said lamely. "Maybe some people are *enjoying* our nature hike."

"Who wants to go back now?" Blane asked, shoving one arm into the air. Seven other campers did the same. Even Ben kind of wished he could raise his hand. He looked around, beaten, at eight expectant faces.

"Well, I . . . all right," he said at last. "Since everybody wants to."

His decision was greeted by a cheer that roused a pair of magpies. They wheeled, screeching, overhead, then disappeared into the trees. Ben's group was heading back down the trail before the birds were out of sight.

"Hey! I go first!" Ben said, scrambling to pass the kids. "And you guys had better do exactly what I say when we get to camp, or from now on we stick to the schedule. No more changes."

That seemed to scare some respect into them. They not only gave Ben the lead position, they trailed him meekly all the way back to the split-log benches at the center of camp.

"Okay, sit here and *don't move*," Ben instructed, feeling a thrill of satisfaction to see the kids actually listening. "I'm going to get our lunches and come right back."

To keep the campers' lunches cool and in reasonably good condition, Peter had devised a system of collecting them all in the morning and passing them out again later. Each group put their lunch bags into a designated plastic crate, and the crates were stacked in the coolest part of the cabin. At lunchtime, each counselor retrieved the appropriate box and carried it out to the benches, where everybody ate. The kids were all supposed to bring drinks in their lunches, to save making a third round of Kool-Aid, so lunch was actually simpler than juice breaks.

"Hi, Jenna," said Ben, sticking his head into the cabin. "I'm just going to grab my guys' lunches and then I'll get out of your way."

"A little early, aren't you?" Jenna asked. She still had a group of girls sitting at the tables for crafts, heavily involved in making what looked like construction paper greeting cards.

"A little. No big deal," Ben said brusquely, hoping he was right. He scurried past her, grabbed the proper crate, and was stepping back out the door when he caught sight of someone emerging into the clearing from the parking lot trail. A leggy, short-haired girl stood at the edge of the woods, looked around a bit as if lost, then began walking toward the cabin.

"Bernie?" Ben breathed disbelievingly.

What was Bernie Carter doing at Camp Clearwater?

Just then she caught sight of him. One slender arm shot up in a wave and she broke into a trot. Ben set his lunch crate on the dirt, waiting for her to close the distance between them.

"Hi!" she greeted him. "Pretty cool camp you've got here."

"Uh, thanks," he said, at a loss.

They stood staring at each other a minute. It seemed rude to ask why she was there, but it was all he could think to say. Bernie seemed to read his mind.

"Lunch!" she said suddenly, rooting through the macramé bag slung over her shoulder. "Elton forgot his lunch, so I brought it for him."

"Boy, he'll be glad," Ben said, taking it from her to add to the box. "He was bragging earlier about what a good sandwich he had today."

"Was he?" Bernie smiled a little crookedly. "So! I was wondering if I'd run into you here. I didn't see you in the library Saturday."

Did that mean she'd been looking? Ben felt a tingle of hope before he remembered he'd told her he was going to be doing a lot of research there that summer, for some imaginary project. At the time it had seemed like a good way to cover his tracks, insurance against the day when he couldn't resist sneaking back there to see her again.

"Oh. Well, I was pretty busy Saturday. You may

have noticed Elton was a little dirty when he got home Friday."

"A little?" Bernie laughed. "He looked like he'd been mixing brownies with a chain saw."

Ben smiled, but whether he was appreciating her sense of humor or her little white teeth he couldn't have said. "Yeah, well, I had to help Peter clean the bus. But it's not like I'll be at the library every week or anything anyway," he added, feeling guilty now about his previous lie.

"Right. Sure."

They stood staring at each other again.

"I, uh, have to get back," Ben said, pointing across the clearing to his group. As far as he could tell they weren't killing each other yet, but he knew that things could change fast. "Do you want to come see Elton?"

"Nah, it'd just embarrass him. Besides, I have to go. See you around, Ben."

She began walking so abruptly that she was already a few paces away before he realized she was leaving.

"Wait!" he called out behind her.

She turned back to face him, a questioning smile on her lips.

"I mean, uh . . . How did you get here?" he asked.

"The bus. I have to hurry or I'll be waiting forever for the next one."

She waved, then trotted off across the clearing,

disappearing into the woods. Before returning to his group, Ben took just a moment to register the thought that Bernie looked cuter in cut-off jeans than anyone he'd ever seen.

"Sorry I was gone so long," he said, beginning his apology the moment he reached the benches. Grabbing Elton's just-delivered lunch off the top of the crate, Ben handed it over. "You forgot your lunch, Elton. Your sister just dropped it off for you."

"What?" Elton opened the bag, peering inside suspiciously. "This isn't my sandwich. I had meat loaf."

"Your name's right there on the bag," Ben said, continuing to hand out lunches.

"I had meat loaf!" Elton insisted.

"I don't know what to tell you." Ben picked up the final bag, only to find ELTON crayoned across it in inch-high letters. "Huh?"

"*That's* my lunch!" Elton said, dropping the bag his sister had just brought and grabbing for the one in Ben's hand.

"That's weird," Ben said, handing it over. "She must not have realized you already had one."

"She saw Mom make it. She watched me put it in my pack. Girls!" Elton added disgustedly, as if that explained everything.

"She must have gotten confused."

"She's confused, all right," Elton agreed.

There had to be some mistake. Why else would

Bernie ride a bus all the way to the lake to bring Elton a lunch he already had?

Unless . . . is it possible. . . ? A thought was forming in Ben's mind, almost too outrageous to consider.

Could she have come to see me?

"What a day!" Leah groaned, slamming her front door. Her parents weren't home to complain about the noise; the last few days they'd been driving all over the state, visiting places they never had a chance to go to when they were working.

Dropping her backpack in the hall, Leah headed straight for the answering machine. Miguel had promised to call her when he got off work at the hospital, and sure enough, the little red light was blinking. She pressed the button eagerly.

"Hi, Leah! It's Shane! It's been a while since we've seen each other, so I was thinking you might want to get together. Call me, all right? I'll be waiting."

Leah's jaw dropped. For a moment she just stood there, listening to the beeps and the tape rewinding. Was he *serious*? After everything that had happened, he thought she'd want to get *together*? She did feel like calling him back, though, if only to tell him exactly what she thought of him.

Not that that ever worked before.

No matter what her intentions, no matter how firmly her mind was made up, Shane had a way of talking her around that was truly scary. She felt a twinge of panic at the mere idea he might work his spell on her again. *Not this time. Not now that Miguel and I have that all straightened out and behind us.*

She hesitated only a second longer before she picked up the phone and began dialing frantically.

"Be there. Come on. Be there," she begged, listening to it ring.

A male voice finally answered, out of breath, as if its owner had just run in. "Hello?"

"Miguel? Miguel, we've got a problem!"

"What kind of problem?" he asked, his tone instantly wary.

"Shane called me."

"He *called* you?" Miguel was angry, and she didn't blame him. "What did the loser have to say?"

"I didn't actually talk to him. He left a message that he wants to get together."

The explosion on the other end made Leah pretty sure Miguel was home by himself. She couldn't imagine him using some of those words in front of his mother.

"Calm down!" she pleaded. "I'm not going to see him. I'm not even going to call him back."

She could hear him taking deep breaths. "Then why do we have a problem?" he asked at last.

"I guess . . . I don't know. I guess I just kind of panicked," she admitted. "Maybe because I'd convinced myself I'd never have to deal with him again."

"I ought to call him back," Miguel grumbled. "I'd be *happy* to meet up with Shane. Anytime, anywhere."

Leah could imagine him twisting a fist in the palm of his hand. "It's better to ignore him," she said. "He just took me by surprise, that's all. It would be like if Sabrina called you now."

There was silence on the other end. Leah's heart double-pumped a beat.

"She, uh, she *hasn't* called you. Right?"

"Noooo. . . . Not exactly."

"Not *exactly*? What, then?"

"She was kind of waiting for me outside after mass yesterday. You know, like she wasn't, only she was? I ignored her, though, so don't worry."

"Oh, right. Don't worry," Leah said bitterly. "That girl's a snake! Just thinking of her touching you makes me sick!"

"And I suppose Shane is Dudley Do-Right."

How could he even compare the two? Sabrina was worse than Shane! Way worse! Leah was so angry and full of adrenaline that she'd have loved to argue that point, but in the end she sighed.

"You're right. They're two of a kind," she admitted. "Too bad we can't hook the two of them up. They'd be perfect for each other!"

There was a long, pregnant pause, giving Leah plenty of time to reflect on what she'd just said.

"Wait a minute . . . Are you thinking what I'm thinking?" she asked.

"You're not going out again tonight!" Mrs. Brewster said from the entryway as Nicole came down the stairs dressed for another date with Noel. "I don't remember you asking me for permission."

"Mom!" Nicole whined, stopping on the bottom step. "I'm seventeen, it's not a school night, and I won't be out past curfew. Why should I have to ask permission?"

"Courtesy, that's why. Maybe I made other plans for you tonight."

"Then maybe you should have asked *me*," Nicole retorted, cowering a moment later at the look that entered her mother's eyes. "I mean, only if we're all supposed to be asking each other and everything," she mumbled, trying to get out of it.

"I thought you were staying home tonight. It might be nice to have a chance to talk to you once in a while."

"But, Mom!" Nicole snuck an anxious peek at the thin gold watch on her wrist. "Noel is going to be here any minute, and it took me two hours to do all this!" She gestured from her upswept hair and magazine-cover makeup to her new pink silk shell and white linen capris—very sophisticated.

"And look," she demanded, holding out both hands and balancing on the bottom stair while lifting one sandaled foot toward her mother. "All new polish to match my shirt. You *have* to let me go."

"I don't know why you couldn't have done something with Noel earlier today. If you aren't going to be a counselor anymore there's no reason—"

"I *am* going to be a counselor! But I don't have to be there every minute, do I? There's all summer for that stuff, and I'm busy right now."

"What did you have to do today that was so important?" Mrs. Brewster wanted to know.

Nicole hesitated. She had *had* to meet Courtney at the mall so the two of them could gossip about Noel and everyone on the cheerleading squad. She had *had* to buy something new and sleeveless to wow Noel with that night. And she had *had* to barricade herself into the bathroom all afternoon to come up with the perfect hair and makeup. Any normal person would understand that. But looking into her mother's eyes, Nicole wasn't sure she was dealing with normal. Her mom had been so touchy lately— even worse than usual—and Nicole had already survived one near miss.

"I was just busy, all right?" she answered at last. "I was out of town all last week."

"I know. Which is just another reason—"

The doorbell rang, interrupting her mother in

midsentence. Nicole checked her watch again, half frantic.

"That's Noel! Mom, you have to let me go. *Please*. I really like this guy, and if I stand him up now . . ."

"Suit yourself," Mrs. Brewster said irritably. "If you think going out with some boy is more important than spending time with your family, then by all means, go."

"It's not like that," Nicole whined, but her mother had left the entryway, retreating into the kitchen so she wouldn't have to see Noel.

Not that I want her to! thought Nicole, quickly coming to her senses. *She's just trying to make me feel guilty. Which I don't! Is it my fault no one ever wants me to have any fun?*

Taking a second to compose herself, Nicole opened the front door. "Hi, Noel!" she said breathlessly, putting on her biggest smile.

"Hey, cutie. Ready to go?"

She floated through the front doorway like the princess he made her believe she was.

"New shirt?" he asked, walking beside her to the driveway. "I like it."

Nicole sighed with happiness as Noel let her into his car. Guy Vaughn had never noticed what she wore, or hadn't liked it if he had. Getting a compliment from Guy had been harder than making the cheerleading squad—which he also hadn't approved of. Noel, on the other hand, was always commenting on her appearance, and he loved the fact that she was a cheerleader. He had already said how cool it would be in the fall if he made senior class president and they were still together. Noel was Guy's opposite in every way.

Nicole was already half in love with him.

"So where do you want to go?" he asked, settling into the driver's seat. "I thought maybe we'd swing by The Danger Zone and see if anyone worth hanging out with was there."

The Danger Zone was the barnlike arcade and pizza parlor that CCHS students considered a mandatory after-game stop on nights when the Wildcats had won. Just the mention of the place sent an excited shiver through her as she imagined herself there in the fall, wearing her brand-new cheerleader's uniform. As a junior, Nicole had been lost in the crowd, invisible, barely able to get a table. As a senior she'd be one of the most important people in the building. She wouldn't mind cruising by there early, just to get a taste.

"Yeah, let's go," she said. "Do you want to get a pizza there?"

Noel shrugged as he backed his car onto the street. "We could."

"And afterwards, let's walk over to that frozen yogurt place on the corner. I've been craving that stuff ever since I got back from camp."

"I noticed," he said, with a sideways glance at her midsection. "Gained a few pounds, haven't you?"

Nicole felt all the air being sucked from the car. She gasped for breath as his words sank in, and her face grew so hot that she had to open a window. She *had* gained a couple of pounds at camp, but she'd managed to convince herself it was mostly muscle. All her clothes still fit. More importantly, no one else had noticed. But now she knew she'd been fooling herself. Noel had noticed. And he wouldn't have said so if it wasn't bad.

"I did, uh . . . I did gain a couple," she admitted, mortified. "But I didn't think it showed."

"Maybe it's just those pants," he said, a slight curl to his lip.

"You don't like them?" she bleated.

"They're fine." He didn't sound as if he meant it.

That's it, she vowed silently. *I'm back on my diet this minute.* She flashed Noel a weak smile, then looked nervously down at her lap. *And these pants are history!*

Thirteen

Peter spotted Melanie all alone in a seat near the back of the bus and walked over to sit beside her. "What's the matter?" he asked.

The campers had settled into the ride with a minimum of ruckus that Tuesday afternoon, exhausted from an entire day of swimming and water sports. After listening to countless hours of whining about how they never had enough time for swimming, Peter had finally gotten smart and given the kids all the lake they could handle. Now, as the bus began the long drive back to town, he could swear a couple of them were already nodding off.

"Nothing's the matter! Why do you say that?" Melanie asked, snapping upright in the seat and flashing him one of her trademark cheerleader smiles.

Or former cheerleader, really. And anyway, it's been a long time since I learned to see through that act.

"I just thought you seemed a little down this week."

He didn't mention the fact that she'd suddenly

taken to riding back and forth in the bus instead of with Jesse, but that hadn't escaped him either. There was something going on between the two of them, and he didn't mean just one of their usual arguments. Jesse was as sulky as Peter had ever seen him, and Melanie was acting as if she didn't see him at all.

"Down?" she repeated, her eyebrows signaling her amazement. "No!"

He just waiting, smiling.

"Well, all right, maybe a little. But I don't want to talk about it," she said. "And anyway, shouldn't you be sitting with Jenna?"

"I will in a minute. You're not going to get rid of me that easily."

"I'm not trying to get rid of you."

Melanie lied as smoothly as she smiled. Normally Peter would have found that unattractive, but her fibs were always such transparent self-defense. He was actually fonder of Melanie than he would have believed possible back in the days before he'd gotten to know her—*really* know her, the way he did now.

"So, how are things going with that study Bible I lent you?" he asked, changing the subject. "Making any progress?"

She grimaced slightly, and he hoped she didn't think he was being pushy.

"I haven't looked at it for a few days," she admitted. "I've been . . . busy."

He nodded. "I only mentioned it because I just

found out my church is starting a new Bible study group in the fall. The woman who's teaching it used to be one of my Sunday school teachers, and she's really sharp. I think you'd like her."

"You . . . you don't mean . . . you're not saying that I . . . ," she mumbled, squirming in her seat.

"Why not? It's going to be all teenagers, and I know you'd like Mrs. Fuerte. You two might really hit it off, in fact."

"I don't think so. I mean, I'm sure she's nice, but . . ."

"It's only a class. And you did say once that you'd like to come to my church sometime."

She gave him an exasperated look. "Do you remember everything I say?"

"Only the important things."

She stared at him a minute. He couldn't tell if she was annoyed, or intrigued, or just looking for some polite way to tell him to forget it.

"Are you going to be in the class?" she asked at last.

"I will if you will," he promised, a smile springing to his lips. "You know you want to. Just say yes."

"I'll think about it," she said, and he could tell she really meant it. "Now go sit with your girlfriend before she gets mad at me."

"We have a reservation under 'Rosenthal,' " Leah informed Le Papillon's maître d'. "I asked for a corner table."

"Right this way, mademoiselle," he replied, gesturing for her and Shane to follow.

"Fancy place!" Shane said, hovering close to her side as they strode through the upscale French restaurant. He seemed underdressed in his sports coat and tie, while Leah looked right at home in the green-sequined evening gown she'd modeled in a long-ago contest. "This is going to cost you a bundle," he added nervously—an unusual tone for him.

Leah smiled. "It will be worth every penny," she assured him.

"Your table, mademoiselle," the maître d' said with a stiff half bow. "I trust this is satisfactory?"

"Very nice." Leah sat in the chair he pulled out.

The man set down a wine list, and Shane took the seat across from her at the intimate table for two. A crystal bud vase with a spray of delicate orchids rested between them at the center of the white table-cloth; the linen napkins were deep burgundy, to match the leather-bound menus with the little gold butterfly on them. The maître d' adjusted the position of a cut-crystal wineglass and ran a critical eye over the positioning of the silverware, making sure everything was perfect before taking his leave.

"They think you're old enough to drink!" Shane whispered gleefully the second the coast was clear. He had apparently gotten over being awed by his surroundings, because the old mischief had reappeared, sparkling in his dark eyes and deepening the dimple in his chin. His black hair was moussed straight back, but no amount of gel could completely kill its waves. Even Shane's hair was irrepressible.

"You *are* old enough," Leah reminded him. "They're just giving me the benefit of the doubt. For now."

"Let's order a bottle of wine," he said, opening the list. "After all, this is a special occasion!"

"It is?" Leah was doing her best to sound calm, but keeping her poise was getting harder all the time. Up to that point she had sailed along on the kind of adrenaline that goes straight to a person's head but leaves her hands completely steady. Now her hands were beginning to shake.

"Of course it is!" he replied. "Are you kidding? Our first real date! I put a lot of work into getting this far, you know."

"I know," she said, not entirely able to suppress the sarcasm.

"I probably shouldn't admit this, but I was pretty surprised when you called to invite me here tonight. I mean, *I* know you ought to want me, but I didn't think I was having much success making that clear to you." Shane flashed his white teeth, clearly delighted with himself. "I should have known you'd cave sooner or later."

She forced another smile. *Just keep thinking that.*

"So what should we have?" he asked, scanning the list. "Champagne? Or do you like red wine better?"

"Order whatever you want, so long as it's not a hundred dollars a bottle. I'm not having any."

"Aw, come on, Leah. They're not going to card you here."

"Wine's just not a big deal to me, and I don't really care to be thrown out of the restaurant. Do you?"

"That's not going to happen," he assured her, acting as if he had plenty of experience in that department. "The worst thing would be that they'd ask for your ID and then you'd say it's in your other purse and then *they'd* say . . ."

Shane's words melted into the background noise as Leah looked up and saw Miguel headed toward her across the restaurant, Sabrina at his side. He looked handsome enough to break someone's heart in the suit he'd worn to the homecoming dance, and the sight of him arm in arm with Sabrina had Leah more than halfway there. Sabrina looked like a movie star with her dark hair swept up in elaborate curls and dangling amethyst earrings emphasizing her violet eyes. She was wearing a floor-length dress cut low enough to show off her substantial cleavage, and the way she threw back her shoulders only made her gifts more obvious. Appreciative heads turned as she walked by, her hips rolling with a life of their own.

Jealous tears sprang to Leah's eyes and burned behind her lashes. She had thought she was ready for this, ready to see Miguel and Sabrina together, but now she knew she wasn't. She would never be ready for that.

"Your table, monsieur," the maître d' said, bowing toward the table next to Leah's. He pulled out a chair for Sabrina, who began to drop gracefully, but halfway to her seat her gaze locked with Leah's and she froze with her rear in midair. Leah heard the intake of breath as Sabrina recognized her. The snake's eyes widened, then darted away, looking frantically to Miguel.

"Uh, maybe some other spot," she hissed, rising back to her full height.

"Is there something wrong with this table?" The maître d' looked shocked. "Is this not what you requested, monsieur?"

"This is fine," said Miguel, walking around to sit in the chair nearest Leah's. "Exactly what I asked for."

"But—but—" Sabrina sputtered, still standing. She glanced Leah's way again, trying to clue him in to the obvious.

"Yes. Hello, Leah," Miguel said pleasantly. "What's the problem, Sabrina? Why don't you sit down?"

"I just thought . . . I mean . . ." She nodded desperately toward Leah.

"You're right," Miguel said, standing again. "It *will* be strange, us all sitting here, at different tables so close together."

Leah could almost hear the girl's sigh of relief. *Wait for it*, she advised silently, trying not to smile.

"Could we have these tables moved together?" Miguel asked the maître d'. "Make it into one big party?"

"Certainly, monsieur."

"Hey, wait a minute!" Shane protested, appealing to Leah. "Who is this guy, anyway?"

Leah smiled sweetly. "Oh, that's right! I forgot you two haven't met. Miguel, this is Shane. Shane, this is Miguel. My boyfriend," she added, unable to resist.

No one said another word as the maître d' pushed the tables together. The moment the man left, Shane broke the silence.

"Well. This is a little awkward."

"How so?" Leah asked, sitting back down. Miguel sat as well, leaving Sabrina standing.

"I just thought . . ." Shane slouched into his seat and dropped his voice. "I mean, since you invited me here . . ."

Sabrina's eyes made the same accusation of Miguel.

"But you knew all along that I have a boyfriend," Leah said innocently. "And Sabrina, I *know* you knew Miguel has a girlfriend."

"Actually," Miguel added, "we thought the two of you might hit it off."

"This is a *fix-up*?" Sabrina gasped. "I can't believe you would do this to me!"

Miguel motioned her into her chair, and Sabrina finally sat down. Leah suspected she needed to.

"It's just that you and Shane have so much in common," Leah told her, full of fake sugar. "You're both cute, single, and incredibly persistent. Not only that, but you're both obviously looking for that special someone who will make your lives complete."

"It just isn't going to be one of us," Miguel said. "We brought you here tonight because we're tired of repeating that. With any luck, you'll really like each other. If not, at least you can have a nice dinner together and trash us after we leave."

He stood up, and Leah did as well, proudly taking the arm he offered.

"You're *leaving*?" said Sabrina.

"You think I can afford four dinners at this place?" Miguel asked, cocking one dark brow. "I'll leave some money for you guys with the maître d', but right now Leah and I have a hot date at Burger City."

"Dressed like that?" Shane demanded.

Leah smiled condescendingly. "After all, it *is* a special occasion."

She and Miguel paused only long enough to leave money for Sabrina and Shane's dinner bill before laughing all the way across the parking lot.

"Geez, that place is expensive," Miguel complained as they jumped into Leah's Cabrio. She had left its top down, knowing it wouldn't be parked long.

"Totally worth it," she declared. "I'd do it again in two seconds, just for the look on Sabrina's face."

Miguel chuckled. "I thought she was going to wet herself. And Shane—he wasn't exactly Mr. Smooth. I don't know what you saw in that guy!"

"Mostly determination," she admitted. "Another quality he shares with Sabrina."

The convertible cruised down the road, the warm night air flowing over them as they laughed, reliving every moment of their triumph. Leah felt as close to Miguel as she ever had, the traumas of the past few weeks finally completely behind them.

"At least it's over," she said, wiping away a tear of relief. "I really think they'll leave us alone now."

"Definitely," Miguel agreed, still grinning. "Even if they don't want to date each other, they sure won't want to see us!"

Fourteen

Melanie was about to follow her campers into the bus Wednesday afternoon when the voice she'd been longing to hear for days spoke up unexpectedly behind her.

"Can I talk to you?" Jesse asked. "In private?"

Her heart leapt into her throat—half dread and half desire. She hadn't spoken to Jesse once since their phone call Saturday night. Not really. Not more than the few words required of counselors at the same camp. She *wanted* to talk to him. Desperately. But not before she knew what to say.

"Now?" she asked uneasily. Half the kids were already on the bus, and the rest were swarming everywhere. Peter and Jenna were directing traffic from the stairs, and both Ben and Leah were riding that day too, since Miguel had pulled another shift at the hospital. It was neither the time nor the place for a private conversation.

"Just . . . give me a minute." Grabbing her by the wrist, he pulled her to the edge of the parking lot, perhaps hoping that the sheltering trees might provide some privacy.

"The bus is going to leave," she protested nervously.

Her ride was far from the uppermost thing on her mind, though. The feel of his skin on hers was so intense that she'd have said anything just to distract herself from the contact. It seemed like a lifetime since they'd last kissed. Her eyes drifted longingly to his lips.

"I'm not going to make you miss your bus," he said. "Although there's no good reason you can't ride home with me."

Melanie shook her head reflexively. "Not a good idea." If she was alone with him, even for five minutes . . .

"Why? *Why* isn't it a good idea?" Jesse demanded, raking his still-damp brown hair straight back with frustration. "This is killing me, Melanie. I'm sorry I ever said anything about you talking to David, all right? I'm sorry I even mentioned it! Is that what you want to hear?"

"It's not about what I want to *hear*. . . ."

"Then what *is* it about? Do you know?"

"Yes, I know!" she retorted angrily. "It's about *us*, Jesse. It's about the way we always end up fighting. It's about discussions just like this one! I don't expect everything to always be easy, but—"

"What *do* you expect? Can you tell me? Because

I can't take this anymore. Either we're together or we're not."

His expression was so tormented that she felt her irritation slipping away. Jesse was hurting. And she was the one hurting him.

"I know," she said with a sigh.

The Junior Explorers' bus rumbled to life. Melanie glanced anxiously over her shoulder, hoping David was going to wait.

"*What* do you know?" Jesse asked.

"I know I have to make a decision. And I'm thinking about it, Jesse. Don't assume this is easy for me."

"No? Well, if you're not enjoying it and I'm not enjoying it, why are we doing it?"

The bus horn honked. She gave Jesse an apologetic shrug and starting edging into the parking lot. "I have to go. They're waiting for me."

"I just want to—"

"Jesse!" she pleaded, torn. "I have to go." She didn't let herself look at his eyes as she turned and started running toward the bus.

"Okay, fine!" he yelled after her. His voice rang through the parking lot, sure to be heard through every bus window. "You want to think about something? Think about this: I love you, Melanie!"

"I can't believe I'm doing this," Mrs. Del Rios said, about to knock on Charlie Johnson's door. "I hope you know what you're talking about, Miguel, or this is going to be very embarrassing."

"He wants to sell," Miguel assured her in a low, excited voice. "I was right here when he said so."

"People talk sometimes," she warned. "If every speech that came from every mouth was one hundred percent accurate—"

The door opened suddenly, startling both of them. Charlie Johnson stood in the doorway hunched over his metal walker, his piercing blue eyes a shock of color against his pale skin and snow-white hair.

"I thought I heard talking out here," he said, a tad suspiciously. "Did you ring the bell? Because if you did, it didn't work."

"No, we were just about to knock," Miguel told him. "You remember me, right? I helped Jesse paint your house."

"I remember *you*," the crusty old man said, looking pointedly from Miguel to his mother.

"I'm Mariana del Rios," she said, holding out her hand to shake Charlie's. "I'm sorry to bother you like this, but my son and I were hoping to speak with you briefly. Is this a bad time?"

Charlie finally smiled, obviously amused. "Well, my schedule's pretty busy, what with watching TV all day, but I can probably spare a few minutes. Do you want to come in?"

Going in was exactly what Miguel was dying to

do. He had been in Charlie's house once before, to help Jesse and Nicole with a Thanksgiving turkey they were trying to cook, but that had been a long time ago—and even then he'd only seen the kitchen for a few minutes. When he'd helped Jesse paint, Miguel had caught peeks through windows here and there, but most of the drapes had been drawn. He hadn't been interested then anyway. He hadn't had a reason to be.

"Well . . . if you don't mind," his mother said haltingly. "I feel kind of silly barging in on you like this. . . ."

"Go *on*, Mom," Miguel whispered, nearly pushing her through the doorway.

Charlie led them into the living room, a dark room made dimmer by the lengthening afternoon shadows. The drapes were pulled shut, and most of the light came from the television. Miguel could see a worn brown sofa and recliner, but his eyes skipped quickly from the furniture to the peeling wallpaper, dingy moldings, and scraped hardwood floor, trying to estimate the time and money it would take to make everything like new again.

Charlie started to reach for a light switch, then changed his mind, perhaps belatedly realizing how shabby the whole room looked. "You know what? We'll be more comfortable in the kitchen," he said, taking a sharp turn toward the other side of the entry hall.

In the kitchen, the three of them took chairs around the big central work table. Miguel perched on the edge of his.

"You must be wondering why we're here, so I'll get to the point," Mrs. del Rios told Charlie. "My son heard you say you might sell your house. We'd like to talk to you about possibly buying it."

"Really?" Charlie made no attempt to disguise his interest. "Without even seeing the whole thing?"

"We will want to, of course, but—"

"Ask him about carrying the paper," Miguel whispered eagerly, earning an annoyed look from his mother.

"I'll be very frank, Mr. Johnson. My husband died of cancer a few years ago. Our family didn't have health insurance and my two children and I were left with a lot of debt. Then I got kidney disease and couldn't work. . . . We ended up on public assistance. I recently received a transplant, though, and now I'm working again. We've managed to save a little money and were planning to move into a private apartment . . . and then my son got the wild idea to buy your house instead. I don't know how much you're asking, but I definitely don't have the down payment. We still won't qualify for a bank loan. I hope I'm not wasting your time even being here," she added, with another sideways look at Miguel.

"Like I said, I'm not the world's busiest guy,"

Charlie told her. "It can't hurt to hear what you have in mind."

"Well, Miguel took it into his head somehow that maybe you'd like to have the monthly house payments made to you instead of a bank, so that you could earn the interest yourself. . . ."

"Carry the paper?" Charlie clarified. "I can see advantages to that, if everything else worked out."

"What are you looking for in the way of a purchase price?" Mrs. del Rios asked.

"Well, let's see. I haven't given it a whole lot of thought. . . ."

The old man scratched his head a minute, then named a figure that sent Miguel's heart dropping to his shoes. They'd never come up with that! It wasn't even that great a house!

But Mrs. del Rios took the number in stride. "Are you planning to make any repairs, or is that as-is?" she asked.

Charlie laughed. "I'm not exactly in condition to play handyman," he said, gesturing to the walker beside his chair.

"I noticed from outside that the roof is in pretty bad shape," Mrs. del Rios remarked. "That's going to cost a few thousand dollars."

"Well, sure," Charlie admitted. "This is an old house. You'd want to get an inspector out here to go over the whole place, make sure you know what you're getting into. I haven't been upstairs in years—for all I know I've got bats roosting up there."

Miguel's mother laughed. "I'm sure it's not that bad."

Miguel wasn't sure at all. Charlie's price had him suddenly looking at the kitchen in a whole new light. When he'd first walked in he'd been too excited to notice the fifty years of accumulated grime on the cabinets; now he saw that they'd all have to be stripped to bare wood and refinished, both above and below the countertops—which would need to be replaced. The home improvement store in Mapleton had ready-made countertops that weren't *too* expensive; Miguel had helped install one with Mr. Ambrosi once, so he was pretty sure he could do it. As his mother and Charlie continued to toss around numbers and terms, Miguel made more mental improvements, too nervous to listen to the negotiations.

I'd rip out all that old baseboard and put in new linoleum. I wonder if the garbage disposal works. . . . Hey, was that window always broken? Then there's the painting, of course. And that range was probably top-of-the-line in the fifties. Oh, man, this room needs everything but the kitchen sink. No, wait. It probably needs that too. What was I thinking? he berated himself, feeling the first creeping tendrils of doubt. *I told Mom this was a good house! I'm the one who dragged her over here when she didn't want to come. I'm the one who said I could fix anything that was wrong. I was crazy! I can't fix all this.*

Well, she just won't want it, he reassured himself. *She'll make some polite excuse and we'll get out of here and never mention the whole . . . was that a mouse? Oh, please, tell me it wasn't. Rosa will freak if the place has mice. I mean, Charlie was just kidding about the bats. Wasn't he?*

Then suddenly his mother was rising from the table. "Do you mind if Miguel and I take a look upstairs?"

Charlie waved them off. "Look wherever you want. Take your time."

Somehow Miguel got his feet underneath him and followed his mother to the staircase. The wooden banister was cracked, the lower end detached from the crumbling wall. The carpet on the stair treads was worn down to the backing.

At the top of the stairs, the hardwood floor lay thick with dust. Mrs. del Rios moved tentatively across the landing to a window. The sill was a fly graveyard, accumulated cobwebs suggesting how at least a few of them had died. Miguel's mother stood looking out over the weedy front yard, apparently stunned into silence.

"I'm sorry, Mom," Miguel whispered, moving to her side. "I know you didn't want to come. I don't even know what we're doing here anymore."

"No?" She turned to him, an unexpected smile spreading warmth from her lips up to her eyes. "It looks like we're buying a house, *mi vida*."

"Your mother and I want to talk to you girls," Nicole's father began on Thursday night. All four Brewsters were in the living room, Nicole and Heather having been summoned to the couch right after dinner. "There's something we want to say."

Nicole could barely keep from groaning out loud as she wondered what their offense had been this time. She had hardly even been home long enough to screw up.

Heather, on the other hand . . .

Nicole could write a book on the subject of her younger sister's failings. Still, her parents wouldn't have asked her there just to hear them yell at Heather—however entertaining that might have been.

"Is this about the phone bill?" Heather asked nervously. "Because I honestly didn't know that was a toll call."

Nicole leaned back into the sofa cushions. Maybe this was going to be interesting after all.

"It has nothing to do with the phone bill," Mrs. Brewster said from the chair opposite the sofa. Her husband hovered behind her, his hands braced on the back of her chair. "We just want—"

"Nicole's the one who broke that glass," Heather volunteered. "She dropped it unloading the dishwasher."

"You little narc!" Nicole squealed. "I ought to—"

"Enough!" their father said sharply. "Will you kindly let your mother speak?"

Nicole reined herself in, but not without one last blistering look at Heather. "Sorry, Mom," she mumbled, hoping her parents would hurry up and get whatever it was over with. Noel was supposed to call later, and she wanted to be close to the phone.

Mrs. Brewster took a few deep breaths, then managed to find a smile. She glanced over her shoulder at her husband, who smiled at her in return. Something in Nicole's gut tensed at the sight.

"I can see you girls think you're in trouble, but you're not," Mrs. Brewster said.

Nicole relaxed an iota.

"Actually, we have some very *good* news to share with you," her mother continued. "Your father and I . . ." She paused and glanced over her shoulder again.

"Your mother and I . . . ," Mr. Brewster said, in that nauseatingly mushy voice he'd been using for weeks.

"The two of us, well . . ." Nicole's mother's smile was so big now that Nicole could see her back teeth. "We're having another baby!"

"*What!*" The word ripped out of Nicole along

190

with the breath that deserted her body. All she could see was a blur of whirling room and her parents, smiling like two demented Cheshire cats. Were they out of their minds?

I must have heard wrong, she thought, praying that was the case. It would be better to go deaf, or to have some sort of weird brain tumor that garbled sound, than to have another sibling.

Look what happened last time! she thought, with a sideways glance at Heather. She half expected to see her younger sister clapping hands or yelling "Goody!" or failing to grasp the situation in some other important way, but to her surprise Heather sat as if frozen on the sofa, her expression as stunned as Nicole's.

"A . . . a baby?" Heather squeaked.

"That's right!" Mr. Brewster replied, with an excess of good cheer. "You're finally going to be a big sister, Heather."

"But . . . but . . ."

"But you're old!" Nicole finished for her. The fact was so obvious—how could her parents not see it? "You're way too old to have a baby!"

Her mother's smile got kind of tight. "Apparently God didn't think so."

"But, Mom!"

Didn't they have any idea how embarrassing this was? Everyone at school was going to find out and know that her parents were still . . . *eew!* Nicole didn't even want to think about that.

"We thought you'd be happy," her mother said.

"*Happy*? Are you *nuts*? This is the most mortifying thing that's ever happened to me in my life!" Nicole shrieked, rising off the sofa.

"Now, Nicole . . . ," her father began testily.

But Nicole didn't wait for the lecture. Running out of the living room, she raced up the stairs and flung herself down on her bed, slamming the door behind her. She hadn't expected to cry, but the tears came almost immediately, hot, angry, and humiliated.

How could they do this to me? she wondered, burying her face in a pillow. She was just starting to get popular at school, just starting to date the A-list guys, just starting to feel good about herself. . . .

Now she'd be the laughingstock of CCHS.

Fifteen

Three whole weeks, Peter thought, breathing a sigh of relief as the campers took seats on the benches for closing assembly Friday. *I survived. Hallelujah.*

"So how are we doing the assembly today?" Jenna asked, appearing unexpectedly at his elbow. "Do you have some sort of schedule or something?"

Over the three weeks camp had been in session, the closing assembly had become more and more of a ritual. It had started out with one or two groups wanting to perform a little skit, or a joke, or a new song they had learned; now it was at the point where every kid wanted to perform at every assembly. And of course they only wanted to perform, not be part of an audience. The whole thing was getting longer and more out of hand than the Academy Awards.

"I don't have a plan," he admitted. "Although I'm probably going to have to start making one. Do you know if there are a lot of groups who want a turn today?"

"There *are* a lot," Jenna said. "And I know exactly

who they are and what they're all doing, so why don't you let me run today's assembly?"

"Gladly!" Not only did that take a load off his shoulders, but it would be fun to sit on the benches, for once, and just watch.

"Okay, go sit down, then," she told him, pointing. "Let's get this show on the road!"

Peter found a front-row seat immediately, but it took longer to get the campers settled down, especially since they all seemed especially wired that day. Eventually Jenna prevailed. Then, to Peter's surprise, she called his own group of boys to the front, along with Melanie's girls.

The combined kids giggled and scuffled on the level patch of dirt facing the benches, jockeying for position. Before the scuffling could deteriorate into full-out pushing, Jenna gave the signal and they all launched into singing:

"Happy birthday to you . . ."

Peter smiled, touched, as the kids finished the song. No one had mentioned his birthday all day. Not even Jenna. He honestly thought she'd forgotten.

Standing up, he applauded the singers. "Thanks, you guys. That was really nice."

But Jenna waved him back down. "Not yet," she said, grinning. "There's more."

The boys from Jesse's and Miguel's groups were now running to the front and forming a huddle, not even waiting for Jenna to call them. Among them they had a few paper bags, which they dug through excitedly, pulling out a mysterious assortment of overlarge hats, shirts, and shorts and putting them on over the clothes they were wearing. All at once, about half the kids broke out of the group, pretending to be swimming in front of the others. At first the swimmers just made silly faces and pretended to splash around, but a couple of seconds later, Joey started yelling.

"Help! I'm drowning! Save me!" he shouted, waving his arms overhead as if sinking under the water. Suddenly the remaining campers broke from their huddle and exploded into a line. And finally Peter understood who they were supposed to be.

"I'm Peter, and I told you not to go out that far!" Mickey yelled, putting his hands on his hips and furrowing his brow. "If you kids would just listen for five minutes, these things wouldn't happen!"

The campers on the benches started giggling, but that was only a warm-up for what was to come.

Elton, wearing red shorts and a whistle, blew an earsplitting blast. "You other counselors save him!" he shouted, pretending to be David. "You know I never leave the dock!"

"*I* can't save him!" Danny yelled in a high falsetto. Somewhere he had found a blond wig and a red bikini top just like Melanie's. "It will take me until next Thursday to get down there from here."

The audience screamed appreciation as it got the joke. Or maybe the kids just liked the hip waggling Danny threw in with it.

"I'm Miguel and I'll get him," Robby announced. "I'm the fastest swimmer."

"No! I'm Jesse and I'm the fastest!" Steve cried.

"I'm faster!" Robby insisted, pushing Steve.

"No, *I'm* faster!" Steve shouted, pushing back.

By now the campers were screaming with delight. Joey continued to pretend to be drowning, while Danny pranced around flipping his blond wig, Elton and Mickey practiced stern looks, and Steve and Robby pushed each other back and forth like two of the Three Stooges. All of a sudden, Jason sprang onto an overturned crate, wearing a whistle, a pith helmet, and mile-wide red shorts.

"I'll save you!" he announced dramatically, with a cartoonish flourish of one arm. "I'm Counselor Ben!"

Jason pretended to dive into the water, then swam all over in the most ridiculous manner possible, making a full loop around the benches. He did the breaststroke and the backstroke; he spouted water into the air like a whale; he did a dead-on imitation of the squint Ben made when water got into his contacts.

"I'm coming!" Jason shouted again. "Counselor Ben will save you!" He started toward Joey. Then, with a quick, sly tug, he dropped his red shorts to the dirt and stepped right out of them.

"Oooh! I lost my bathing suit! Save me!" he cried

over the hysterical screams of the other campers. He had his own shorts on underneath, but anyone would have thought he was truly naked from the reaction he got. The campers howled and whistled and clapped as if it was the funniest thing they had ever seen. Peter tried not to laugh, to spare Ben's feelings, but even Ben was cracking up by the time Jason finally rescued poor Joey, pretended to drag him to shore, then ran off to hide his supposedly naked self behind the drinking fountain. Miguel and Jesse beamed proudly from the sidelines, unwittingly revealing Jason's source for the bathing suit incident.

After at least five rounds of bows, the actors finally returned their seats. Then the last group came up: Leah's girls.

"We have a song to sing for Peter too," Chelsea announced in a shy voice. "Everyone can sing with us."

"For he's a jolly good fellow . . ."

Peter felt himself blushing. By the time the girls got to the end, all the campers had joined in, howling the last *"Fell-el-oooooooooooooow, which nobody can deny!"*

Amy walked forward and handed Peter a paper grocery sack decorated with red hearts and yellow flowers. "There's cards in there from everyone," she said. "But *our* group made the bag."

Peter reached in slowly and removed a card from

the top, an uneven brown paper square with a soccer ball and baseball bat painted on its front.

Dear Peter, he read silently. *Camp is the best. You are the best. Yore friend, Jason.*

"They all say pretty much the same thing," Jenna told him proudly, reading over his shoulder. "The kids love camp, and they love you, too."

"Wow. I . . . I wasn't expecting this." The words on the card blurred a bit and he blinked hard. "They really like it?"

"No, they *love* it," Jenna repeated, grinning.

Suddenly a chant rose from the back. "*Ice cream, ice cream, ice cream!*"

"Oops," said Peter, grimacing at Jenna. "I don't know where they got the idea there was going to be ice cream."

"Probably from the ice cream." Jenna's smile grew as she turned and pointed across the clearing.

The other counselors had snuck to the cabin during the final song, and now they were walking back to the benches. Jesse and Miguel each held one end of an open ice chest, the eerie fog spilling over its rim giving away the dry ice inside. Behind them, Ben and Melanie balanced two big platters of cupcakes.

"Who wants ice cream?" Jesse shouted, snatching an ice cream bar from the chest and tossing it into the crowd. Kids dove frantically, bumping heads and trying to push each other out of the way.

"Whoa!" Jenna said. "I'd better take charge of

passing those out before we end up with casualties." She started to hurry off, then turned and dropped the lightest kiss beside his ear. "Happy birthday, Peter," she whispered.

"It is!" he called after her.

Finding out the kids thought camp a success was the best present he could have gotten.

It's not that big a deal, Ben coached himself, hesitating outside Bernie Carter's front door. *You just say, "Bernie, would you like to go out with me now? I thought we could catch a movie."*

Sounded simple.

Yeah, simple-minded. What kind of loser shows up at a person's door and expects her to go on a date with him right then? I should have called first.

He had planned to, actually. But the Carters' phone number was unlisted—unusual in Clearwater Crossing—and he hadn't figured that out until he'd arrived home from camp that afternoon.

I could have called Peter. He would have given it to me. Probably. Peter could be a stickler about anything related to the kids.

So there Ben was, standing on the Carters' front step in his good shirt and khakis, with the sweatiest palms he'd ever had in his life.

It's now or never, he thought, raising a hand to knock. He cocked his fist back and brought it forward, only to watch it screech to a halt a half inch from the door. *Never*, he decided. *Am I completely crazy?*

He was halfway back down the walkway when Bernie opened the front door.

"Ben?" she called. "Ben, is that you?"

He stopped, then turned very slowly, his heart pounding halfway out of his chest.

She must have seen me from a window, he realized. *She must have seen me standing outside her door, then watched me slink off like a total geek.*

"Bernie! Hi!" he said, sounding more natural than he would have thought possible. "I was about to knock and then I realized my wallet wasn't in my pocket. I was just on my way to check the glove compartment to make sure I had it." His knees were actually shaking, but his words were so smooth that he dared to believe she wouldn't guess that.

"Why do you need your wallet?" she asked, walking barefoot down the path to meet him. She was wearing a sunny yellow gauze dress with a colorful inch-wide assortment of beads around one ankle. Nothing about her smile suggested she didn't buy his story.

"Well, I need it to drive, for one thing. My driver's license is in there."

She nodded. He took a deep breath.

"And I wanted to make sure I had my money before I asked you to the movies tonight. On a date," he added clumsily, to make sure there was no mistake. He'd done the just-friends movie with Angela Maldonado, and he couldn't take that type of disappointment again.

"Well, I . . . I . . ." Bernie's gaze had dropped to the sidewalk. She seemed suddenly fascinated by her pink-painted toenails.

Here it comes, he thought. *She's going to say no.*

"If you don't want to go, it's cool," he said quickly, trying to cut his losses. "I know it's short notice. I'll just—"

"No! I want to go," she interrupted. "It's just . . . well . . . this is kind of embarrassing, but I have to ask my mother. Wait here, all right?"

Before he could manage a reply, she spun around and ran back into the house, her gauzy skirt flying out behind her.

Did she . . . did she just say yes? Ben asked himself, stunned.

He felt as if he needed to sit down. Instead, he shuffled the rest of the distance to the curb and leaned against the roof of his mother's car, which seemed a lot more manly than dropping his khaki-coated rear to the sidewalk. He wanted to be sure his posture set the right tone when Bernie came back out.

Please, please let her mother say she can go! Ben thought, throwing his request out into the universe for anyone who might be listening. *If things keep going this well, I could actually end up with a girlfriend!*

* * *

"This is so unbelievable," Melanie murmured, lifting her lips from Jesse's. They were lying on a blanket in the wild grass far behind her house, lost to everyone but each other. The stars overhead curved toward the horizon as if pasted inside a giant bowl, their combined light so bright she could see Jesse's features.

"What's unbelievable?" he asked, his lips brushing against hers.

"This. Us." She tightened her embrace, burying her face in his neck. "I know this is what I want now."

He chuckled ironically. "If it wasn't, I'd be looking pretty stupid."

When he had yelled out after her at camp on Wednesday, any chance of keeping their feelings secret had been blown away in the same breath. Especially since she had waved the bus onward without her, staying with Jesse instead. The campers who dared had been teasing them for the past two days, and even though no one in Eight Prime had said anything directly, Melanie had been the recipient of countless significant looks and smiles. Jenna and Leah in particular were obviously dying for details, but Melanie wasn't sharing. Yet.

Soon, she promised herself, bringing her lips back to Jesse's. *I just want to keep this for myself a little longer.*

Her hands traveled through Jesse's thick hair; her

body pressed against his. Now that she had finally given in to her feelings, even an hour without him was torture. She only felt whole in his arms.

She remembered a movie she'd seen once, about a woman who believed couples were split apart at birth, destined to spend their whole lives looking for each other. Only the really lucky ones ever got matched back up.

Melanie kissed Jesse again and knew she was one of the lucky ones. For the first time in her life, she felt like Melanie Andrews—the fortunate, privileged creature everyone thought she was, not the unhappy girl she'd always seen when she looked in the mirror. Her eyes closed as Jesse's kiss deepened. Her tongue traced his teeth, wanting to memorize every part of him.

And then Jesse pulled away.

"You still haven't said it," he told her, tension creeping into his voice.

"Said what?" But she knew. She could feel her spine stiffen, his anxiety seeping into her.

"What I said to you. At the bus. You never said it back."

He wanted her to say she loved him.

"Well, I didn't think . . . I mean, here we are . . . ," she fumbled.

Did he really need her to say it? Wasn't it obvious?

He pushed a strand of hair out of her eyes, the gesture so tender it nearly broke her heart.

"I love you, Melanie," he told her. "Say you love me, too."

Fragments of memories whirled through her mind. In her entire life she had only ever said she loved three people: One was dead now, one was an alcoholic, and the last had taken what he wanted and dropped her cold. Jesse was asking for so much more than he realized. If she opened up, if she gave him this part of herself, she could never take it back—he could only take it from her. Melanie gulped down a shuddering breath. There couldn't be many more pieces of her heart left to go around.

"*Do* you love me, Melanie?" he asked, a worried edge to his voice. "Do you? Just say yes."

She held him so tightly she could feel both their hearts beating, thundering in their chests. Just the feel of him, the smell . . .

She took one last breath, for courage.

"Yes," she whispered, her lips barely grazing his ear. "I love you something awful."

Find out what happens next in Clearwater Crossing #18, *Prime Time*.

About the Author

Laura Peyton Roberts is the author of numerous books for young readers, including all the titles in the Clearwater Crossing series. She holds degrees in both English and geology from San Diego State University. A native Californian, Laura lives in San Diego with her husband and two dogs.

Get a Life

When a classmate is diagnosed with leukemia, the students at Clearwater Crossing High organize a fund-raising carnival. But after they've formed teams to work the booths, the members of one group find they couldn't be more different. There's aloof Melanie, the girl who has it all . . . and wannabe Nicole, who wishes she did. Best friends Peter and Jenna jump at the chance to make a difference, while football jock Jesse sees a perfect opportunity to impress. Brooding Miguel keeps to himself . . . to the frustration of confident Leah. And tagalong Ben? He just wants to make some friends.

Soon the carnival is over, and the surprisingly close-knit team members drift back to their regular lives. Then an unexpected tragedy strikes. Will the eight friends come together again . . . or is it time to say good-bye?

Reality Check

Jenna and her friends are having a car wash to help needy kids. There's more in the autumn air than soapsuds, though. . . .

Leah and Miguel are trying to keep their new love a secret . . . but a heartbroken Jenna is the first to find out. And if her over-before-it-began romance isn't bad enough, her younger sister Maggie is driving her crazy! How can Jenna have a life when she's sharing a room with the enemy?

Peter's got a crush too—on Jenna! He doesn't want to ruin the special friendship they share. Is telling her the truth the answer?

Nicole's determined to win a national model search. It would be sweet payback to conceited Jesse for humiliating her at school. But payback doesn't quite fit with Nicole's resolution to be a better person—does it?

Clearwater Crossing #2, *Reality Check*, is on sale now from Bantam Books.

0-553-57121-4

Clearwater Crossing

Heart & Soul

Heart & Soul

After a cheerleading stunt goes terribly wrong, Melanie is rushed to the hospital. Her frightened friends are praying for her recovery. Drifting in and out of consciousness, she feels a comforting presence. Is her imagination at work, or is Melanie not as alone as she thinks?

Of course Nicole is concerned about her so-called friend, but she has a modeling contest to worry about. She's still following a strict diet—she's got to be in perfect shape. Especially now that Jesse's begun to take her seriously.

Jenna finally has a room she can call her own! She loves its privacy, its spaciousness. But will her new surroundings cause hurt feelings between Jenna and her closer-than-close sisters?

Clearwater Crossing #3, *Heart & Soul*, is
on sale now from Bantam Books.

0-553-57124-9

Promises, Promises

Halloween is around the corner, and Eight Prime is
putting in a lot of hours working on a spooky haunted
house fund-raiser. It's the perfect opportunity for Leah
and Miguel to bring their budding relationship into the
open. So what is Miguel so afraid of?

Jesse's off the football team—maybe forever. If he can't
convince Coach Davis that he's given up drinking, he can
give up his NFL dreams for good. Jesse's ready to promise
the coach anything to get back on the Wildcats. But
promises can be hard to keep. . . .

Melanie would never have believed she'd be interested
in a do-gooder like Peter. Yet lately he's the only thing she
thinks about. Not that she's falling for him, or anything
dumb like that. She and Peter would make a terrible
couple. Wouldn't they?

Clearwater Crossing #4, *Promises, Promises*, is
on sale now from Bantam Books.

0-553-57127-3

Just Friends

Bonfires, pep assemblies, and *football:* Spirit Week has kicked into high gear at Clearwater Crossing High! All Nicole can think about is getting Jesse to take her to the homecoming dance, but he's not in a partying mood. Nothing matters now that he's off the Wildcats.

Everything matters to Jenna these days. Dealing with her sisters, earning good grades, getting over Miguel . . . more than ever, Jenna needs a friend she can count on. She needs Peter. But has her best friend in the world found someone he likes better?

Ben is on a mission—to fit in! He thought being part of Eight Prime would solve all his problems, but he's still invisible at school, and his new friends don't really seem to accept him. Then Ben hits on a plan. If he can pull this off, he'll be the toast of CCHS!

Clearwater Crossing #5, *Just Friends*, is
on sale now from Bantam Books.

0-553-49258-6

Keep the Faith

Ever since her mom's death, Melanie has dreaded the holidays. This year, though, she's got to put on a happy face: Amy, one of the underprivileged children she's been a friend to, is spending Thanksgiving weekend with her!

When a kidney becomes available for Miguel's ailing mother, he drops everything to be by her side. In a moment of desperation, he vows he'll do anything, *anything*, if only his mom will get well. Will Miguel have the chance to make good on his promise?

Now that Eight Prime is *this* close to buying a school bus for needy kids, there's no further reason for them to stay together. Nicole's ecstatic: She's free! At last she can go back to her regular life. The funny thing is, she doesn't really want to anymore. . . .

Maybe achieving their goal isn't the end . . . just the beginning of everything else.

Clearwater Crossing #6, *Keep the Faith*, is
on sale now from Bantam Books.

0-553-49259-4

New Beginnings

Amid the hustle and bustle of preparing for Christmas, Nicole can barely find a moment to breathe. She can't wait for winter break—until her parents drop a big bombshell. . . .

Melanie's last-minute holiday plan is just a teensy bit complicated. First, she needs to keep it secret from her dad, and second, the scheme involves a major-mileage road trip. Will Jesse's sleek BMW come to her rescue?

Peter and Jenna have dreamed up the best gift ever: winter camp for the Junior Explorers. But the fun stops short when an Explorer disappears . . . and Eight Prime must find the child before it's too late.

Clearwater Crossing #7, *New Beginnings*, is on sale now from Bantam Books.

0-553-49256-X

One Real Thing

Not only did Melanie fail to set things right with her family, she did what she swore she never would: She let Jesse into her life. Now that she's opened the door, slamming it shut could prove to be a losing move.

Ben's never kissed anyone . . . and it's starting to really bother him. He's determined to get his first smooch by the new year's end. How hard can it be?

Leah's got to make up her mind whether or not she'll compete in the national finals of the modeling contest she reluctantly entered. Being in front of the camera isn't her thing, but she can't turn down a chance at a scholarship and a free trip to California with her friends. Can she?

Clearwater Crossing #8, *One Real Thing*, is
on sale now from Bantam Books.

0-553-49257-8

Skin Deep

Good-bye, Clearwater Crossing . . . hello, California! Well, at least for the weekend. The girls of Eight Prime are on an all-expenses-paid trip to the Golden State, and each of them has her own agenda. . . .

Leah's trying to focus on the modeling competition—and the scholarship that goes with it. But how can she strut down the catwalk when all she can think about is Miguel's marriage proposal?

Melanie's ready for sunshine and fun, forbidding herself even a moment's thought about Jesse. So why is it that everywhere she looks she sees his face?

Jenna's squeezing in as many cool sessions as possible at the Hearts for God youth rally. She wants Nicole to join her, but her starstruck friend is too busy keeping her eyes peeled for movie stars—and hoping to be discovered. Will Nicole give faith a chance . . . or is Hollywood calling her name?

Clearwater Crossing #9, *Skin Deep*, is
on sale now from Bantam Books.

0-553-49260-8

No Doubt

Every time Jenna gets involved in Caitlin's life, she makes things worse. How could she have revealed her shy sister's crush on Peter's handsome brother? And now that she has, how can she earn back Caitlin's trust?

Just because she got in a little trouble, Nicole's parents have found her a job—at the restaurant where her perfect cousin, Gail, works. Nicole is less than thrilled to be around such a Goody Two-shoes until she discovers that Gail isn't quite as good as she remembered . . . or as all the adults seem to think.

In an unguarded moment, Miguel proposed to Leah. He'd have said anything to keep from losing her. But now that she seems on the verge of accepting, he's on the verge of panicking. Is marriage really the answer?

Clearwater Crossing #10, *No Doubt*, is
on sale now from Bantam Books.

0-553-49261-6

Prime Time

Miguel is having the summer of his life. Helping out at the day camp, working at the hospital, and spending every spare minute either alone with Leah or goofing off with Eight Prime is the most fun he's had in years. To top it off, he and his family are about to move into a house of their own. Can life really be this good?

Jesse can barely believe that he and Melanie are finally together. So how can he leave her? Sure, he promised to visit his mother in California, and Melanie promised to visit her aunt Gwen . . . but can't they get out of it somehow?

Nicole's mom is having a baby! How could her parents do this to her? Don't they know how embarrassing this will be for her at school? More importantly, don't they realize they could all end up with another Heather on their hands?

Coming in June 2001!